Street MOGULS

&

Mafia BOSSES

By

Tony Steele

Felony Books, a division of Olive Group, LLC,
P.O. Box 1577, Belton, MO 64012

ISBN-13: 978-1541372153

Felony Books 1st edition January 2017

10 9 8 7 6 5 4 3 2 1

Manufactured in the United States of America

For information regarding special discounts for bulk purchases, please contact Felony Books at felonybooks@gmail.com.

Street
MOGULS

&

Mafia
BOSSES

Books by Tony Steele

RICO
RICO 2
RICO 3
RICO 4
TRAP-A-RELLA
TRAP-A-RELLA 2
TRAP-A-RELLA 3
TRAP-A-RELLA 4
FULL JACK MOVE
OF MY DREAMS

www.felonybooks.com

Prologue

1992

The lighter shook in Jerome Branson's frail, dark-skinned hand as he fought to strike it. He inhaled a deep breath to steady his nerves. If this was the same dope he copped a couple days ago, he had all the reason in the world to be trembling as bad as he was. The last time he shot up this quality of heroin, he nearly puked up his guts. He usually didn't earl after he shot up—only when he got some really good dope.

After a couple nervous deep breaths, Jerome struck the lighter and a flame popped up, as if his prayers had been answered. He let out a long sigh of relief and slid the flame back and forth under the spoon, liquefying the heroin.

***

A two-tone Delta 88 pulled to a screeching halt at the curb, catty-corner from a dilapidated apartment complex. The group of young men who sat out front passing a single 40-ounce bottle of Old English among each other, paid the car no attention. They assumed the car belonged to someone who was looking for a fix or maybe the warm lips of a hooker. It wasn't unusual to see an unknown car parked or cruising the streets of the neighborhood. The building was located in one of the worst neighborhoods on the Northside of St. Louis.

But if they only knew who the man was sitting in the car watching them …

His name was Ares. He was the most feared man to run the streets of St. Louis. Among the criminal underworld he was known as Mr. Death, a hitman for hire. Those whom he was contracted to kill never lived long enough to regret whatever they did to the person that hired him.

This was the case with the heroin junkie, Jerome Branson, that Ares had been commissioned to kill. Jerome had robbed the gambling house of the Barozzi crime family. When word got back to them that a junkie was responsible for the robbery, they hired Ares to send a serious message to anybody foolish enough to make the same mistake.

Ares picked up the .22 revolver in the passenger seat and screwed on a silencer. He opened the door and climbed out of the Delta 88, stuffing the pistol into his back, then pulled down his shirt. He strolled toward the apartment complex with the swagger of someone who belonged here.

***

As soon as the heroin began to course through Jerome's veins, he felt his stomach knot up. Before he could draw the syringe from his arm, his mouth began to fill with the hamburger meat he ate earlier. He grabbed the tin bucket sitting next to the couch and puked. He kept the bucket there for emergencies like this. He knew his chances of making it to the toilet in time was next to impossible.

Certain he had puked up the last of the burger, he eased back into the dingy cushion of the couch. Spit dribbling for his lower lip that he didn't bother to wipe away; instead, he groped himself.

He needed a good nod before he shot up the rest of the half of gram and go on the hunt for his partner-in-crime. His partner had short-changed him out of his share of the cash from the gambling house they had robbed a couple days ago.

Before he could really get into his plan to get his fair share of the robbery, the thought faded from his mind. The bliss of his high had kicked in and he slipped into a nod.

***

Almas Branson, just a scrawny pre-teen boy with an unwashed t-shirt, stared with hate-filled eyes through the ajar door at his father, Jerome Branson, who had pumped his veins with death again. He hated the fact that his father was addicted to heroin, because his habit was affected Almas. Almas's father shot up every dime he could get his hands on, forcing him to turn to the streets to provide himself with the basics—food, toothpaste, toilet paper, clothes. Even with him earning his own money, his father still managed to shoot up what he hustled.

He always gave Jerome whatever he had scrounged up in the streets without any argument. Except for today. Almas was two weeks away from the beginning of the school year and he didn't want to begin the year as the dingy kid. So to avoid having his classmates picking on him the entire semester, he started working for the dealers in his neighborhood as a watcher or a runner. In the three days he had been doing this, he accumulated over seven hundred dollars—enough to keep him in fresh gear for the entire school year. So there was no way he would let Jerome get his grubby hands on his hard earnings. Not a single dime.

Allowing his father to get fully into his nod, he slowly pushed open the door and tip-toed into the apartment. The front door would squeak when closed all the way so he gently pushed it near-shut, stopping it before the spring latch touched the faceplate. He didn't want to wake his father.

A couple steps was all he managed to take when Jerome's eyes suddenly popped open. "Where is it, boy?" he asked in a long drawl, his left hand held out.

"What?"

"Don't play stupid with me, boy. You've been out there hustling with those niggas all day."

"You're right. I have. That's why you ain't getting shit. *I've* been out there hustling, not you."

"What the fuck you say to me, boy?" Jerome slowly sat up and stared coldly at his son. He had killed men for saying no to him. There was no way he would let his flesh and blood tell him no.

"I suggest you finish stuffing that shit in your veins and leave me the hell alone," Almas said, lacking any emotion in his voice.

"Nigga, you must've forgot who the fuck I am."

Jerome sprang to his feet and his knee struck the edge of the coffee table, knocking over the heroin he just copped.

The rage he was feeling made him foam at the mouth. If he never did anything else with his life, he would succeed in one thing—beating his son to death. He picked up the lead pipe laying on the side of the couch.

At that very instance, Almas had enough. He suffered too many beatings with the lead pipe his father was now clenching, enough beatings to last a lifetime. This was where he'd put an end to the abuse. He reached under his shirt for the .380 one of the dealers he ran with gave him.

***

Ares, aka Mr. Death, dug the .22 revolver out of his back and approached the red-painted door. Suddenly three sharp pops went off—*Pop-pop-pop!* He had been in the business for too long to not know what that sound was and what it meant for his intended target.

He reared back his leg and slammed his foot into the door.

It flew open.

The sight that greeted Ares when the left him speechless. A young boy no more than twelve stood over the body of the man he was here to kill. The boy held a smoking gun. It wasn't what the boy had done that shocked Ares; it was the expression on his face. Ares knew what that look was. It was one of a killer. A natural killer. Truly, a rare find.

"Son, what is your name?"

"Almas Branson. And yours?" Almas asked as he whipped the .380 toward Ares without taking his eyes off of his father's lifeless corpse at his feet.

Ares trained his gun at Almas's head. "My name is Ares."

"So, Ares, you were coming here to kill my old man? And me too, I guess?"

A chill went up Ares's spine as Almas spoke. His words were void of emotion. Ares knew that Almas had no feeling left, probably hadn't felt emotion in years. Almas was a heartless child who had the thirst for blood now.

"No, I wasn't here to kill you," said Ares. "I was contracted to kill your father. No one else."

"Since the job is done, you can leave."

Ares stuffed the revolver into his back. He had been wanting to find someone he could instill his skill into, and Almas had the potential to be that individual. The answer to the question he was about to ask Almas would determine if he would kill Almas or take him under his wing.

"I have what you need to quench that savage thirst coursing through you now. You want it?"

For a moment Almas stood silent, staring at his father's dead body. He couldn't disagree with Ares. Murdering his father sparked a craving in him to end somebody else's life.

Anybody's life. Since Ares promised to give him that satisfaction, he would go with him.

"Okay then," said Almas. "Let's go."

Almas tucked the .380 back into his waistband, then turned from his father's body as if he was nothing more than a stain on the carpet. He followed Ares out the door.

Chapter 1

23 Years Later

A mixture of burnt orange and yellow sunlight ascending over the horizon showered Almas's brown skin as he stood in front of the full-length window. The beautiful scene didn't evoke any emotional reaction out of him. His well-chiseled frame stood completely still, like a statue.

It wasn't until the sun finally made its voyage over the horizon did Almas move, turning from the window and heading to the bathroom for a quick shower. He found himself thinking about Ares more than he had in years. He hadn't seen the old man since his first professional hit when he turned eighteen. He just might have to call him up to see how he was doing. If it wasn't for Ares, he wouldn't be living in a six-figure penthouse with a bank account holding more money than he could spend.

And he wouldn't be one of the most sought after professional assassins in the country.

He made a name for himself as being the best of the best—the elite. Sixty people fell victim to his skills of killing, ranging from crack dealers to government officials, including his own father. It wasn't just his ability to kill, but how he did it that made him so profound. Ares spent seven years training him in several forms of martial arts, hand-to-hand combat and a wide range of weaponry. If there was a way of killing somebody, Almas Branson knew how to do it.

As he was just about to step into the bathroom, his iPhone began to ring. He fetched it out of his sweatpants pocket and answered it. "What's up, Ellison?"

"Are we cool?" Ellison asked, referring to the security of the phone line.

The need to answer Ellison's question would be a waste of breath. Ellison wouldn't be able to call him if the line had been tapped. He had his smartphone set up to detect interference and give out a busy signal. He knew Ellison asked him the pointless question just to get a reaction out of him.

"Yes," said Almas. "We're cool."

"Good. I have a job for you this morning. All the information you need has been passed on to your friend."

"Okay. I'll talk to you once the deed has been done."

"See you then."

Almas hung up his phone and began to strip off his sweats for a shower, before he stepped out to bring about the end of another life.

***

Almas Branson brought his black metallic Porsche 911 to a screeching halt at the garage doors on Morganford Road. Slowly, the garage doors opened and he pulled the 911 into the mechanic's garage.

A young man in navy blue coveralls who looked to be no more than twenty-five was sitting in a chair in the garage, playing an online video game from his phone. His name was Nathan Branson. He looked up when he saw the Porsche 911 park in its usual spot next to his Mazda Enfini RX-7, a vehicle that car lovers would see drifting the streets of Tokyo. The young man quickly switched his phone screen off. Almas would have a fit if he caught him playing video games while on the clock. Nathan began to pretend he was doing some work; he started wiping off grease from some of his tools.

Little did he know, Almas knew he was fucking off. Nathan had left clear evidence: his table was cluttered with empty energy drinks and protein bar wrappers. It was all Nathan ate while he spent countless hours gaming.

"Nathan, what did I tell you about playing your games while on the job?" said Almas as he climbed out of the Porsche wearing a black Ermenegildo Zegna suit.

"I'm sorry, AB, but this guy I've been playing against has been kicking my ass ragged." Suddenly, an idea hit Nathan. He snapped his fingers. "How about we kill—"

Almas cut him off. "No."

"You don't know what I was about to say."

"Because I'm not interested in it. I'm only interested in today's job."

"Okay. This is what we got today."

Nathan glided his fingers across the keys on his laptop. Almas watched Nathan locate the information on his latest target. Nathan was the only one out of his family he dealt with, and the only one Almas had ever committed a murder in front of. Everyone else was either drug addicts or law-abiding citizens.

Nathan was a technological genius as well as one of the world's greatest hackers. He had a high IQ, but he didn't use his mind to further mankind. Instead, when he was younger a local meth dealer used Nathan's skills to evade the law, as well as a few other things. When Nathan's mother found out what her son was doing, she begged Almas to help free Nathan from the dealer's clenches. Almas did exactly that— by killing the meth man and a lot of his associates.

To assure Nathan never fell in the wrong hands again, Almas took him in as somewhat of an assistant. He possessed the kind of talent that came in handy in his line of work, like obtaining information about the man he was hired to kill.

"Here we go," said Nathan, turning the screen toward Almas. "Your guy is Seymour Morgenstern, a senior partner at a financial company. He was cleaning the money for a Mafia family out of Chicago, until he started to dip his hand in the cookie jar. This attracted the attention of the Feds. They were planning to arrest him to get him to flip on his former business partners."

"Did he hire any protection?" Almas asked, still reading Seymour Morgenstern's profile.

"From the security footage, yeah. I ran facial recognition and discovered they're a group of mercenaries out of South Africa. Ex-Delta Force soldiers."

"And housing?"

"Let's say Fort Knox doesn't have anything on this place."

"I guess I'll be going in as a delivery man."

"I kind of figured you would say that." Nathan pointed to a brown khaki uniform, fake ID card, and the package at the head of the table. "The package has a P-95 with a silencer, and the van is ready to go." He motioned with his thumb to the white van parked behind him.

"Despite your game addiction, I see you're still on top of your job this morning," Almas said as he peeled off his suit jacket.

"You know me, Mr. Multitask. *And* I get lucky every once and a while."

Almas's blank expression made Nathan smile. It always astonished Nathan how unemotional his older cousin was, a characteristic he loved. The blank murderous faces fit Almas perfectly, especially with him being a contract killer and all.

Chapter 2

The receiver nearly dropped out of Seymour Morgenstern's hand. What his lawyer told him drowned his face with fear. He had embezzled $17 million from the Rossini Crime Family. When Gerald Rossini, the boss of the family, found out his transgression, he threatened to kill him. Seymour wanted to take it as nothing more than tough talk. But he wasn't about to stake his life on an assumption. Seymour took the necessary precautions to assure they wouldn't succeed in killing him. But all that had changed after he was just informed by his lawyer of the possibility of the FBI arresting him. He was certainly a dead man.

Seymour hung up on his lawyer by pressing a button that connected him to his secretary. He quickly gathered his composure and spoke: "Sarah, I need you to cancel all my appointments for the day. I have some business to attend to."

"Yes, Mr. Morgenstern."

"And Sarah, call up my pilot and tell him to fuel up the jet. I'll be there in twenty minutes. And I need you to see if Mr. West is in."

"At once, Mr. Morgenstern."

Seymour hung up the receiver and began to stuff what belongings he had into his briefcase.

A slender-built bodyguard named Mr. West entered the office and stared coldly at Seymour, who was nervously dialing in the combination to the wall safe located behind his desk. Despite his hatred of Seymour, the kind of money he paid him and his men as personal bodyguards kept his Glock holstered on his hip. If it wasn't for that, he would've put a bullet in Seymour's head and been done with him.

"Your secretary said you wanted to see me."

Seymour continued to stuff his briefcase as if West wasn't even in the room. "Tell your men we're leaving."

"Where to?"

"I'll explain when we get on the jet."

West nodded and headed out of Seymour's office.

***

Almas pressed his finger to his ear as he eased off the brake and onto the gas pedal, accelerating the van down Market Boulevard. "Nathan, I'm two minutes away."

Nathan's voice came through the earpiece crystal clear: "And … I'm … in. The eyes in the sky are under my control, so you're clear."

Almas removed his finger and took hold of the steering wheel with both hands, as he turned into the underground garage.

***

Agent Byron Avery took a glance over at his partner, Agent Sheryl Dunbar. She had her face buried in the file of the man they were coming to arrest like usual. She was the typical hardnose federal agent—all work and no play. She was always trying to prove herself. It was like if she didn't take the job serious, her credibility as a good FBI agent would be destroyed.

"I'm interested to know, Sheryl … what would you do without life as an agent of the Federal Bureau of Investigation?"

Agent Dunbar let out an irritable sigh. She didn't want to start the morning off with his senseless questioning about how she did her job. She carried out her duties as a federal agent exactly how she was trained, with professionalism and conviction. She didn't treat the job like it was fun and games, like her partner and other agents did. They dealt with some of the country's most hardened criminals, and that same hardness was an image they had to reflect.

"The way I do my job isn't what's important right now. Just keep your eyes on the road."

"Yes, boss," Agent Avery replied in a sarcastic tone. Then he switched the blinker on and steered the Dodge Charger onto Market Boulevard.

***

Sarah, Seymour's secretary, let out a long yawn. Her one-year-old son spent the better part of the night crying. It wasn't until she and her husband decided to take him to the emergency room did they learn that their son had an ear infection. They didn't leave the emergency room until the wee hours of the morning. Coffee was the only thing keeping her eyes open, and it was starting to run its course.

She waited a few minutes with her hand on the receiver. When Seymour didn't page her asking for anything else, she bounced to her feet, nearly knocking over her chair. She quickly made her way to the restroom, just as the elevator door slid open.

The two men sitting in the lobby peeked over the rim of the newspaper they were reading and eyed the man stepping off the elevator. He wore a brown khaki outfit with a cap pulled low, shielding his eyes. The two men weren't liking the vibe they were getting off him; they stood with their hands on the Glocks that were holstered on their hip.

Almas didn't give them a chance to ask questions or draw their weapons. He stuck his hand into the slit cut in the package he carried and yanked out the P-95 concealed inside.

Before the bodyguards realized the delivery man wasn't who he appeared to be, he was firing off several kill shots— one to the head and two to the chest.

Seymour nearly dropped to his knees when he heard the glass coffee table in the lobby break. "Shit! They're coming for me!"

The sound of shattering glass didn't elude West either. This was what he hoped for, some action. He unholstered the Glock 19 from his hip. "Seymour, stay down," he ordered, and proceeded toward the door.

Without being told twice, Seymour dove behind his desk. It would be where he would stay until West came to get him.

West motioned to the man who stood outside of Seymour's office to go to the left, while he went to the right. His plan was simple: they would box in the person coming to kill Seymour, and the perfect place to execute it was where they were heading. It was the section of the office where the cubicles were located, an easy place to hide and pick off their target without him even knowing they were there.

Almas knew he couldn't play this cat and mouse game with them. The odds were against him. He knew they were trying to box him in. He would have to use it to his advantage.

He grabbed a stack of papers from the desk tray and tossed them in the air. He backed out of the cubicle and slid into the one beside it. He laid flat on the floor, waiting for his prey to walk into his trap.

The paper flying in the air immediately drew West's attention. He signaled to the man coming up the aisle with him to move in. The man nodded and crept toward the cubicle that the papers flew out of.

Almas listened closely to the approaching footsteps and took aim with the P-95, where he anticipated his intended target to step into his line of sight. He inhaled a deep breath as the bodyguard in a dark suit walked into his view.

Almas squeezed the trigger.

The shot was dead on, striking the man in the temple. He fell backward through the opening of a cubicle across from the one Almas was concealing himself in. Almas propped himself up on one elbow and placed two more shots into the bodyguard's chest. He wanted to be certain the man never got up again.

As quickly as he took out the second bodyguard, he swung his firearm toward the cubicle he had used as bait. He fired five shots through the wall, not giving the next body-guard a chance to react. Suddenly, a loud thump echoed from the other side, followed by a loud moan of someone in pain. Almas knew he had hit his mark.

He got to his feet and eased out of the cubicle. He crept up to the opening with his weapon ready for a gun fight, in case he was walking into a trap. It wasn't. The body-guard on the other side of the wall was sprawled on the floor with three bullets in his chest. He was still alive.

West coughed up a glob of blood as his cold eyes glared at the man who had shot him. "You bastard ..."

Almas looked away, firing a slug into the man's face. He headed toward the office to complete his job.

When Seymour heard the door to his office open, he breathed a sigh of relief. He rose from behind the desk, expecting to see Mr. West. "You sure have earned your ..." The words faded from his lips as he stared down the barrel of a gun. Before he could swallow the lump of fear clogging his throat, Almas squeezed the trigger.

The wall behind Seymour caught the blood splatter. Seymour dropped to the floor like a bag of sand.

In the same fashion Almas had guaranteed his kills with the bodyguards, he stepped over Seymour's body and pumped two shots into his chest. It was one of the many lessons Ares drilled into his head: *Never assume. Always be certain your target is dead.*

Nathan's voice came in Almas's earpiece: "Almas, you need to get a move on it. The Feds are on their way up."

"I'm on my way down," he replied, tucking his gun into his back. He rushed out of the office.

***

Agent Dunbar leaned against the wall of the elevator with her arms folded over her chest and stared impatiently at the numbers slowly counting up to the tenth floor. She was ready to get this arrest underway so she could begin with her interrogation. Interrogating a suspect was the part of her job she really loved, and Seymour Morgenstern was about to be another addition to her collection of suspects broken by a female agent.

The elevator stopped its ascend on the tenth floor and the door slid open to a woman screaming at the top her lungs. Agent Sheryl Dunbar saw what the woman was ter-rified about—there were two dead men in the waiting area.

Dunbar and Avery drew their government issued Glock 23s and approached the woman.

"Ma'am, what happened?" Agent Avery asked.

"I don't know. I was in the restroom."

Agent Dunbar looked back to the elevator and noticed the second elevator heading down to the underground garage. "He's headed to the garage!" Dunbar ran toward the emergency stairs. "Byron, radio for backup. I'm heading down to cut the guy off."

"Sheryl, wait!" Avery protested, but she was already shoving her way through the door. "Shit!" He unhooked his walkie-talkie from his hip and brought it up to his mouth. "Agents need backup at the Bratex Building on Market Boulevard!"

***

Quickly, Almas headed toward the delivery van when Nathan's voice came booming through his earpiece. "A.B., you have an agent headed your way!"

"Fuck," Almas mumbled. A shootout with a federal agent wasn't something he wanted. He had to take the agent down without taking a life in the process. An agent's death was the kind of heat he didn't want on him.

He stepped behind a concrete pillar and waited.

Agent Dunbar burst through the emergency door nearly out of breath. She inhaled a deep lungful of air to settle her rapid breathing, then she exhaled. Her dark brown eyes slowly combed the area for the murder suspect, as she cautiously began her search.

As flat as Almas could press his back against the concrete pillar, he listened to the footsteps grow closer. He suddenly stepped out once the agent was within striking distance. In one swift motion he knocked the Glock from her hand and pounded the butt of the P-95 into the back of her neck, rendering her unconscious. She collapsed into his arms, as her gun went tumbling a couple feet away.

He sat her down and propped her up against the pillar. He searched her, finding her service pistol strapped to her ankle. Pocketing the palm 9mm, he retrieved her Glock. He jacked the round out of the chamber, ejected the clip and tossed the Glock into the agent's lap.

"A.B., you have a few minutes before backup arrives," Nathan said.

"I'm heading out as we speak. I'll see you at the dump spot."

"See you there."

With one last look at the unconscious agent, Almas cut his gaze away and headed toward the delivery van. Under any other circumstance, he wouldn't mind trying to get with the young and beautiful agent. But this wasn't one of those situations. The job, and keeping himself out of prison, came first. Love was secondary.

He climbed behind the wheel and started the van up.

The sound of screeching tires echoed throughout the garage as the van speed off toward the exit ramp.

***

"This is *not* how agents operate!"

The deep roaring voice of Special Agent-in-Charge,

Lewis Day-Bailey woke Agent Dunbar out of her uncon-scious state. She knew he was about to give her a piece of his mind for her reckless actions that nearly resulted in her losing her life. She sucked in a deep breath and braced her-self for it.

Agent Day-Bailey barged his way through the agents that were talking among themselves and searched the crowd, which was a mixture of agents and civilians. When his sights locked in on the person he was looking for, he let out a low growl and marched up to Agent Dunbar, who was being attended to by paramedics.

Agent Dunbar tried to defend herself first. "Listen, Lewis. I had to race down here before our suspect got away."

Day-Bailey said nothing. He stood there, biting down hard on his bottom lip. The top of his head, where hair had once grown, was turning cherry red as if it was about to explode any minute. "Agent Dunbar, we'll talk about this later. Right now, get yourself to the hospital and have your-self checked out."

"Yes, sir," she replied, as paramedics helped her into the back of the ambulance. She let out an audible sigh. At least she had a couple hours before he brought the hammer down on her.

Chapter 3

"In today's news, rap artist Trey Bryant—also known as 3B—is being released from prison next month, after serving three years of a five-year sentence for rape in the first degree. The world is asking the question: When will he drop his highly anticipated album?"

Trey Bryant switched off the television and stepped over to the sink, which was a part of the all-in-one toilet. He picked up the battery-operated beard trimmers and began to cut off his dreadlocks, one lock at a time. He wanted to step out of prison a changed man, literally.

This was the day he had dreamed of for the last couple years. The three years he had served so far on his five-year sentence was the worst thing he had ever experienced in his entire life. Despite the environment he grew up in, where men like him were expected to be behind bars, he was unable to accept that reality as easily as others.

He wanted to be the first person from his 'hood who didn't see the inside of a prison. So instead of jumping in the dope game or gangbanging, he turned to music. But obviously that didn't help. Eventually he landed himself behind bars, and this stint nearly killed him. He had been getting into fights with the inmates and guards, causing so much ruckus the administration was forced to put him in the Protected Custody Unit.

PCU was where he was being released from today.

"Ay, Trey-Dog!" his neighbor Stanley Cody screamed from the cell next door to his.

"Hold on, old nigga. I'm trying to cut off the rest of my wig," Trey yelled back up into the vent just above the sink/toilet combo, also known as the "prison cell phone." It was how the forty cells communicated with each other, since they spent nearly 17 hours locked down. Other than recreation, library, showers, phone calls and chow, they never left their one-man cell.

"C'mon, nigga. It's some shit I want to drop on you before you bounce," Stanley whispered.

"A'ight, old nigga."

Trey ran the trimmers over his head one last time to be certain he had gotten all the hair. He knew what Stanley Cody wanted to rap to him about. Since he was sent to PCU a year ago, Stanley had been putting him on point, calming him all the way down—and at the same time Stanley was schooling him so he wouldn't come back to prison like most guys with short bits. Some inmates never took full advantage of their incarceration by learning from it, nor improving themselves as men, as human beings.

It was the kind of game Trey could put to use to help him grow his rap career to the heights he had always expected it should be. He wanted to get Stanley out of prison as well. Stanley was serving life without plus fifty years for killing his best friend.

Coming up in St. Louis in the '70s was hard. If a person wasn't part of the working force, he made a living hustling in the streets. That was exactly how Stanley and his childhood friend Lee survived. They peddled dope for one of the city's biggest heroin pushers, Fat Ronnie. It wasn't long before the game that made Fat Ronnie 'hood rich turned on him and had him shooting up the very product he sold.

Stanley and Lee didn't let their former boss's addiction stray them. They got with his connect, scooped up his clientele, and became the new bosses of St. Louis. But it didn't take long for the game to switch on them, pitting them against one another. Their rivalry got so heated it escalated to gunplay, eventually pulling Stanley's baby mama into the beef. Lee gunned her down when he mistook her for Stanley while she drove his car.

This sent Stanley on the hunt with his pistol in hand and murder on his mind. It didn't take long for him to find

Lee hiding out at the local pool hall they sold heroin out of when they were younger. He didn't say a word to Lee, just walked right up to him and shot him execution style.

That day the game claimed three lives—Lee's, Stanley's, and Stanley's one-year-old daughter.

Trey cleaned the locks of his dreads out of the sink and stepped onto the toilet. Though he stood six-foot-two, the vent was still a couple inches higher. "What's up, Stanley?"

"You remember everything I told you?"

"No doubt."

"Good. Now remember, I'm counting on you to go out there and handle your business."

"Come on, playboy. Don't play me like that. You know I gotcha." Trey knew what Stanley was referring to. His now-grown daughter, Safiya. She hadn't spoken to him in the last 27 years of him being incarcerated. She felt she had nothing so say to him. He left her alone at a time in her life when she needed her father the most.

If there was one thing Trey would do for Stanley when he got out, it was reconnecting him with his daughter. That was his one sole purpose above all other things, other than getting Stanley out of prison.

There was yelling going on between prisoners that Trey learned how to block out. But when the noise suddenly fell silent, he noticed. The wing door had opened and a guard entered the bay. The guard approached cell 108—Trey

Bryant's cell—and pointed a finger at the number on top of the cell door, a signal for his co-guard working the control panel.

"Stanley, they're here," said Trey.

"A'ight then."

Trey hopped off the toilet and began to pack up his stuff. Other than his television, CD player, and prison-issued clothes, he really didn't have much of anything to pack up. A few minutes was all it took to pile everything he had in the plastic tubs they gave prisoners to store personal items and canteen in.

The guard wheeled a cart up to the door to load Trey's tubs on. Trey inhaled a deep breath when the door opened, then he walked over to cell 107 and knocked on the window. He waved for the old man with a head full of gray hair to come to the door.

Stanley Cody counted off his last set of push-ups and bounced to his feet. He rolled his wide shoulders as he strolled over to the door. For him to be in his late forties, he had the physique of a middle-weight bodybuilder. Eighteen-inch biceps shaped his arms, and a muscular chest and stomach seemed to act as a shield. Trey was always amazed by the way Stanley was built. Stanley was the reason Trey worked as hard as he did to tone up his body. The kind of body Stanley had was what made A-List stars, which was one of Trey's goals now that he was a free man.

"Now remember what I said, Trey Dog."

"Damn, nigga. For the millionth time, I got you."

"A'ight, lil' nigga. I was just making sure we're good, so calm your ass down."

The guard let out an impatient sigh as he folded his arms over his chest. "Come on, Mr. Bryant."

"Damn, man, a'ight," Trey said over his shoulder, then turned his gaze back to Stanley. "You be easy, Stanley, man."

"You know I will, baby boy." Stanley held a clenched fist to the glass.

Trey brought his fist up to the window and pounded his with Stanley's. This might be the last time he saw his friend. Suddenly he shook off the thought, because he was sure it wouldn't be the last time. He was going to make sure of that.

He gave Stanley a goodbye nod, then pushed the cart behind the guard toward the door.

Chapter 4

There was no shade covering the prison parking lot as Nita Candy climbed out of the rear of the stretch limo Hummer. The midmorning sun beamed down on her milky smooth caramel skin, making her even more gorgeous. She had the looks of a lingerie model and a body to compliment her. The cherry red Dolce & Gabbana mini skirt appeared to be airbrushed on her 36C breasts; it accentuated her flat stomach, wide hips and huge butt.

The prison guard staring at her from across the parking lot nearly ran into a parked car. Even when he finally looked up before colliding into the back of the car, he still kept his eyes on her.

Nita Candy flashed the man a snooty look. She was almost tempted to give him the finger. She hated when men stared at her as if she was no more than a piece of meat. Besides, he was beneath her, a pathetic guard who wasn't worth her time. The thirty thousand dollars he made a year was barely enough to pay for the panties that kept her pussy warm.

Men like him were nothing but dead weight, never amounting to nothing more than what they were, the same kind of men her older sister was stuck with. If a man couldn't buy her the world, she didn't have a word to say to them.

"Slip, what time is this nigga supposed to get out," Nita said to the driver.

"I dunno," Slip replied.

"Damn, nigga. What the fuck is you good for if you don't know when this nigga is getting out?"

Slip locked his jaws tight, keeping what he wanted to say to himself. He knew if he told her the thought that crossed his mind they would start arguing. He wanted to avoid bickering with her by all costs. His partner was getting out today and he didn't want him walking out of prison into a heated argument with Nita.

Nita smirked, knowing Slip wouldn't give her any back-talk. Not when her man, Trey Bryant aka 3B, was getting out any minute now.

If there was any man she loved more than life itself, it was 3B. She had been his girlfriend since middle school. Unlike other rappers' girlfriends whose boyfriends kicked them to the curb once they became superstars, he kept her by his side. So in return she remained dedicated to him and his career, through the hard times, the cheating, and now prison.

She was becoming impatient as she rested a hand on her wide hip. Then the prison gate slid open and Trey Bryant stepped through.

He gave the navy blue Hugo Boss sports jacket a confident tug and strolled toward Nita, who was running up to him. She leaped into his awaiting arms and kissed him passionately. He grabbed her soft butt that seemed to soak up his hands.

"I see somebody wants to make this a day I won't forget," Nita said, after parting her lips from his, feeling his erection slithering up her lap.

"Oh, believe me, you won't."

"Then let's get out of here so we can get this party started." Nita took Trey by the hand and escorted him to the Hummer.

"Slip, my nigga." Trey held out his arm to embrace his childhood friend, but then caught himself. He didn't want to give Slip a hug with an erection. "That might not be a good idea."

"Oh yeah. I'm feeling you, my nigga." Slip bumped fists with Trey instead.

Trey dug a piece of paper out of his pocket and handed it to Slip. "That's our first stop."

"What do you mean 'our first stop'?" asked Nita. "This better not be one of those funky hoes you met while in prison."

Slip let out a frustrated sigh. He had love for Trey like a brother. They had been friends since they were in the first grade, and no matter what—right or wrong—he stood by him. But when it came to Nita, she was a decision he didn't stand with. Slip saw Nita as a leech, sucking the life out of his friend.

With Trey being fresh out of prison he hoped his friend finally saw Nita for what she truly was.

"Listen, Nita," said Trey, "I'm not going to start this with you. Not today."

By the seriousness of his tone, Nita knew this wasn't some floozy they were going to see. It was best she kept her mouth shut. She didn't want to piss him off and have him refusing to take her shopping.

"Whatever," she said. "Let's handle this business you gotta take care of so we can get you ready for your Welcome Home party."

Nita opened the rear door and waved Trey inside.

The way Nita waved him in, Trey knew she still had an attitude. He felt a headache starting to come on. She usually caused them when she got into her little funky moods, like now. He sighed loudly, preparing himself for a long ride to Stanley's daughter's job.

"You can act like a real kid sometimes," Trey said as he climbed in the Hummer.

"I know, but you love it," Nita replied sassily. She really wanted to tell Trey off. But she flopped into the soft tan leather seat next to him, slammed the door closed and tried her best to keep calm.

Chapter 5

The group of young men standing in front of the convenience store eyed the charcoal black Porsche Panamera as it pulled up. Its Giovanna rims and Pirelli tires matched the body perfectly. This wasn't the typical car that cruised their 'hood. Heavy-hitters in the game who pushed whips like Porsches rarely ventured this deep in the 'hood with their expensive vehicles. A Panamera would make the heavy-hitters a target to every hungry hustler looking for their next come-up.

But none of them—nobody in St. Louis, as a matter of fact—would have mistaken the young man driving the expensive luxury car as a meal ticket or a come-up. The Porsche belonged to Charlie Owens aka Charlie Hustle, one of the biggest rappers to fall out of their neighborhood. It wasn't just his rap status that kept everybody at bay, but who he pushed heroin for—a man named Pop.

Pop was one of the biggest heroin suppliers in the city. He also had a crew of young shooters who made sure he stayed top dog. So when the corner boys at the convenience store saw the Panamera, they knew to give it a pass.

Charlie Hustle rose from behind the wheel and slid on a pair of Ray-Bans. He hung up his cell phone he was yelling into, then stuck it in his pocket. He strolled around to the passenger side.

"What's up, Charlie Hustle?" one of the young men said.

"Chilling, my man," Charlie Hustle replied, paying the young man no attention. He hated when he had to make a drop-off to Pop. It was always someone who wanted him to listen to their demo tape or put them on. He was a rapper/drug dealer, not a talent agent. He left that job to the professionals.

It wasn't just them hounding him about deals that got under his skin; it was the way they eyed his girl, Stacia. She was the sort of woman a baller would keep on his arm. A real head-turner with a dark chocolate complexion, juicy butt and shapely hips which enhance her looks.

Charlie Hustle opened the passenger door as Stacia unseated herself from the leather seat and stood to her five foot eight height without any help from Charlie Hustle. She slung the straps of her Gucci bag over her shoulder and started toward the store.

Charlie Hustle gripped his crotch as he stared at Stacia's plump butt along with the young men; it jiggled wildly, her skin tight denim jeans trying hard to contain it.

She displayed a sassy expression, which Charlie Hustle truly loved. She wasn't clingy like most celebrity girlfriends. She didn't need to be. She carried herself in a way that said he was her man.

There was nothing in this world Stacia wouldn't do for him. She was the true definition of a ride-or-die chick.

"C'mon, nigga," she said. "It's some shit I want to drop on you before you bounce."

Charlie Hustle fell in step behind Stacia into the convenience store.

"What's good, Biggs?" Charlie Hustle said to the man behind the register.

"Chilling, baby boy," the heavy set clerk replied in a voice as if he had smoked too many packs of cigarettes. He reached across the counter and gave Charlie Hustle some dap.

"Is Pop here?" Charlie Hustle asked.

"Yeah. He's in the back," the clerk replied, turning his head toward the back office.

"A'ight." Charlie Hustle strolled through the aluminum swinging door that led to the storage room Pop had converted into his personal office.

Stepping into the back office was like entering a different world. The room was decorated in the latest furniture and technology. It was the kind of office a Wall Street broker would have.

Poppa Jones, aka Pop, sat behind a black glass desk raking his fingers through his greasy perm. He was from the backwoods of Fairhope, Alabama, a small town where he ended up getting the sheriff's wife and daughter pregnant. When the sheriff learned what Pop—the local gigolo at the time—did, he put a posse together to string him up by his neck. Not wanting to become another casualty of a town lynching, he escaped to St. Louis to peddle pharmaceutical pills called T's and Blues for his cousin Lee.

It didn't take long for him to graduate to heroin, seeing that it was a more lucrative business than his current hustle. As the cash flooded in, so did the ugly side of the business; the competitiveness of the game pitted friend against friend, and it was Stanley Cody who came out victorious, leaving him to lay Lee to rest.

He didn't want his reign over the heroin game to be cut short by a friend like his cousin. So he surrounded himself with the most dangerous killers in the city, killers that held the vultures at bay. It was why he maintained a tight hold on the heroin game in the Lou since Lee died in the early '80s.

Pop rose from behind the glass desk and copped a seat on its round edge. He cockily threw back his shoulders and stared at Charlie Hustle and Stacia sitting in the leather box-shaped armchairs in front of him. If there was anybody out of his squad of dealers who was his biggest earner, it had to be Charlie Hustle. His entertainment clientele alone brought in a little more than two million a month. That was why he invested nearly five hundred grand toward Charlie Hustle's rap career, and the cops protected his investment. He wanted their partnership to last long and be very profitable.

"What do you got for me, baby boy?" Pop asked.

"A half ticket." Charlie Hustle motioned to Stacia with his eyes glued on Pop. He was the kind of man Charlie Hustle always kept a watchful eye on. Over the fifteen years he had been hustling for Pop, he had seen him kill a couple of his own dealers merely because he had the power to.

As unpredictable as Pop was, it wasn't the sole reason Charlie Hustle stayed leery of him. Pop didn't survive as long as he did by being stupid. If a person showed any indifference or backed him into a corner, he would kill them without a second thought.

Charlie Hustle's mother had died at the hands of Pop because of this mistake. He had pumped her veins with a hotshot when she discovered her only child, Charlie "Charlie Hustle" Owens, was selling dope for him. She threatened to snitch him out to the cops if he didn't put an end to her son illegal employment. Instead of succumbing to her demands, he decided to silence her.

Charlie Hustle knew Pop had no idea he blew through a quarter million dollars to learn that it was Pop who had killed his mother. Charlie wanted it to stay a secret until the time was right.

Stacia held out the Gucci bag with an attitude. "Silky Smooth," she said to one of the men sitting across the room, "would you please?"

Silky Smooth, the brown-skinned man sitting on the sectional sofa with four other men, pushed himself to his feet, pulling his maroon Brioni sports jacket snug against his muscular frame. He strolled over to Stacia without a second look. He grabbed the bag from her and tossed it to one of the young men. Silky Smooth was in every sense a killer. He didn't party or date, unless he was required to kill somebody. Other than that, he stayed at Pop's side.

"Pop, why do we have to always go through this?" asked Charlie Hustle.

"Because I don't deal in doubt," Pop replied. "I deal in certainty."

After counting, one of the young men said, "We're good, Pop."

"Now was that hard?" Pop asked Charlie Hustle.

Charlie ignored Pop's comment. If there was one thing he despised about Pop it was his condescending attitude. It was one of the reasons he couldn't wait to put a bullet in his head. "Since we're good, I'm going to bounce. Herb is throwing a coming-home party for 3B. So I need to get to the crib and dress."

"A'ight then. You should have mail when you arrive at home," Pop said.

"Cool." Charlie Hustle rose to his feet and gave Pop some dap. "I'll see you next week."

"Sure you will," Pop replied.

Charlie Hustle headed for the door with Stacia tagging close behind him. He waited for Pop to say something smart as he always did. But nothing was said. Charlie Hustle was glad. With 3B getting out of prison today, the label would put all their attention toward pushing him and his new album. That meant Charlie Hustle would be put on the back burner like usual.

Playing second fiddle had Charlie Hustle pissed off. He was so upset, ready to snap, so he was glad Pop didn't say anything smart. He knew he would have lost it, and right now wasn't the time to lose anything—it would only get him killed.

Pop had to die, so Charlie Hustle couldn't allow his hatred for 3B to rob him of the chance to kill Pop. He took a deep breath, then pushed through the swinging door and walked out of the office.

Chapter 6

More than anything, Agent Sheryl Dunbar's pride was hurt as she angrily tapped her fingertips against the desktop. She didn't like the idea that somewhere on the streets of St. Louis was somebody who had gotten the drop on her. The thought ate at her so bad, she was planning to spend the rest of the day at the shooting range to release her frustration.

If it wasn't for her and her partner having to finish up the report on the incident, she would've been out the door and at the range right now.

"Sheryl, don't let this bother you," Agent Byron Avery said.

Agent Dunbar tossed her pen to the side and stood up. She snatched her sports jacket off the back of her chair and headed for the elevator. She knew it was coming. Agent Avery would never let her live this down. He had labeled her a hot shot, and this was the kind of label he dreamed of rubbing in her face. But she wasn't going to give him the pleasure. She would rather listen to her Glock popping off shots than him telling her how she needed to stop being so gung-ho.

As Dunbar reached the elevator, Special Agent-in-Charge Lewis Day-Bailey motioned her and Agent Avery to his office. "Over here, guys," he said. She hoped he wasn't calling them to his office to get on her case about the incident that left her knocked out and their suspect, Seymour Morgenstern dead. If this was the case, she knew she would be leaving his office with a two-week suspension for losing her cool.

She inhaled a deep breath, trying to get her emotions in control. She headed toward his office to receive her scolding with grace.

***

Almas pulled in front of the old gothic Catholic Church and eased from behind the wheel of the Porsche 911 with confidence, as he slid on a pair of Versace sunglasses and strolled toward the church. St. Vincent was the oldest church in the city, dating back to the mid-1800s. It was where Almas's handler, Ellison Eaton, worked out of.

As unusual as it was for his handler to commission the death of countless people here, Almas saw it as genius. No one would ever suspect a priest to be the handler for a professional killer. Besides, if the cops were to learn he was a handler by some unforeseen reason, he had the church to shield himself behind.

Almas trotted up the short steps and took the handle of the door, when it suddenly came open.

A woman in her mid-forties ran into him with her face buried in the screen of her smartphone. She looked up from the text she was reading, startled. "Oh, I'm sorry," she said.

"No problem." Almas moved to the side.

"Thank you," she said as she cut around him and galloped down the steps, bringing her attention back to her phone.

Almas stuck his hands in his pockets and entered St. Vincent, basking in the brief moment of the woman's soft body against his.

***

Smoke oozed from the 50-year-old Ellison Eaton's nostrils as he leaned back in his crusted velvet chair. The call he received an hour ago was a handler's worst nightmare. It seemed that Almas's most recent job had put him on the FBI's radar. They were an agency that he or Almas didn't want chasing them, especially when one of their people was harmed in the line of duty. They spared no expense to bring those type of perpetrators to justice.

The incident was the reason he called Almas to meet with him today. He knew Almas wouldn't want to hear what he had to say. But it was in their best interest to put things on hold until the heat died down.

They would be unable to take jobs for a few months to a year. Ellison was certain Almas would start to become restless. He needed something to occupy his time until they could get back to what they were good at. Then, moments ago, a visit from an old friend's daughter may have solved that problem for him. He just hoped Almas would do it.

Ellison sat up and dumped the ashes off his cigarette.

"You don't have to tell me," said Almas knowingly. "I know the last job had peeked the Feds' attention."

"It has, so we gotta put things on hold for a moment."

"Well, at least I can finally take that vacation you've been hounding me about."

"Not quite." Ellison smashed the cigarette out in the ashtray. "There is one more job I need you to do for me."

"Sure. What?"

Ellison began to explain the visit he just received from the daughter of his childhood friend, Jared. After graduating high school, Jared had gotten into the music business while Ellison enlisted in the military. The man worked his way up from being an assistant to owning a popular record label in ten short years. When he and his partner landed a deal with a major distribution company a few years ago, it took their local company worldwide. His co-founder forced him to sign over most of his shares in the label as soon as the company became one of the top companies in the music industry. The emotional stress of being forced out of the very company he helped build contributed to his failing health, which eventually claimed his life. His daughter paid her father's ex label owner a visit to get what was owed to her father. Instead, she got a gun to her head and she was warned to never seek payment for her father's stake in the label again.

Fearing her father's ex-partner might decide that she posed a threat to his empire and have her murdered, she turned to Ellison for help. Now he was giving Almas the task of bringing about the end of this man's life to protect her life, and her family's lives as well.

"Here." Ellison tossed some papers in front of Almas. "That is a contract. The guy I need you to kill is Herbert Wolff. He is the owner of Wolfgang Records. Get him to sign it before you kill him." He picked up the pack of Dutch cigarettes and shook one out. "It'll make you the legal owner of the record label." He fired up the cigarette and took a couple drags off of it, then tapped the ashes into a glass ashtray on his desk. "Mr. Wolff usually meets his mistress,

Dasha, at the Hilton around this time of day. It's the most likely place to wack him."

"Does he usually keep any security with him during these rendezvous?" Almas asked.

"From what I have been told, no. You should have no problems getting in and out."

"Seems simple."

"It is." Ellison sat the half-smoked cigarette in the ashtray, and with a slight tilt of his head he said, "I assume you already know you can't kill this guy in the usual manner."

"Yeah. It goes without saying."

"Then there is nothing else needed to be said."

Almas was glad Ellison had procured the deal for the record label. He knew he would become restless within a month and would want to get back to what he did best—killing.

"This won't fall back on us?" Almas asked. He had to put the question out there, as irrelevant as it was. Ellison was the best at what he did because of his DC connections, and because he was thorough. Especially with the FBI incident on the last job, Ellison would be extra thorough with this current one.

"Come on, Almas. I've been doing this too long to be careless."

"I know. My bad." Almas stood. "I'm going to get out of here and get started."

"You know, I'm a phone call away if you need anything," Ellison stated.

"You best believe I will," Almas replied as he headed toward the door, bidding Ellison farewell with two fingers in the air.

Ellison grabbed the cigarette out of the ashtray and continued to smoke as he slumped back in his chair. He wanted to get in one last smoke before evening services started.

Chapter 7

Jermaine "J-Money" Irons's dark hands appeared to belong to a gorilla. They roughly squeezed the caramel butt cheeks riding him. The seductive moans and the ass bouncing against his lap got him so aroused his dick started to hurt. He understood why Herbert Wolff had put a ring on her finger at seventeen. Chloe Wolff's sex game was superb.

"Fuck me, J-Money!" she screamed, as she rode his thick arousal.

"What the fuck you think I been doing for the last two hours?" he replied.

He had been putting his dick in every one of her pleasure holes ever since he got to this hotel. He had filled her up with so much cum, he expected her to explode any minute. She took every drop without showing any signs of backing down. He was going to continue giving it to her as long as she could take it.

Chloe felt herself about to reach her third orgasm. She braced herself for it, clawing her fingers into her own breasts. She knew this orgasm was about to be the finest of them all. J-Money was the only man who could make her pussy gush in the way it did now. Though her husband, Herbert, sucked her pussy in a way no man ever had, he didn't have what J-Money had between his legs. But even if Herbert was hung, he wouldn't have known how to give it to her as good as Jermaine "J-Money" Irons.

J-Money ignited a nostalgic pleasure in her that she had longed for since the night she got her cherry popped when she was thirteen. Her boyfriend back then was hung like J-Money, and he beat her pussy up every chance he got.

The mere thought brought Chloe to a breaking point. She bit down on her bottom lip and really began to grind on his dick, shoving every inch inside of her. Then it came; she climaxed along with him, collapsing onto his sweaty chest, exhausted.

"Herb must've pissed you off," said J-Money. "That's the only time you fuck like this."

"Yeah. He's talking about putting me on an allowance because I spend too much," Chloe said.

"What does he expect? You're a high-price bitch."

"I see you know me." Chloe sat up, resting her hands on J-Money's brawny chest. It wasn't just his dick game that really intrigued her; it was his looks as well. He was a handsome man that any woman would love to have, and he was all hers—in body and mind. "So, J-Money, you gave any thought to what I asked you?"

J-Money tried to avoid Chloe's alluring hazel eyes. He was the founder and CEO of Gatz Records. Prior to music, he lived the life of a robber and an occasional drug dealer. His past put him on guard constantly, especially with anything involving a crime, because the Feds were always looking for a way to bring down the guys that they felt "escaped." What Chloe was suggesting—a contract killing—would be just the charge the Feds needed to lock him away for life.

Chloe wanted J-Money to kill her husband, Herbert Wolff. This was something she relentlessly nagged him about for a couple months now, but he wouldn't cave in to her demands. J-Money had his own plan in motion to bring about Herbert's death, but not because she asked him to.

"Herbert's death is something we don't need right now," J-Money told her. "It would attract the kind of attention we don't want."

"That excuse is starting to become the theme nowadays," Chloe pouted, as she rolled off the top of J-Money and strutted into the bathroom.

J-Money didn't care about Chloe catching an attitude. He wouldn't let her or anybody send him to prison for the rest of his life. The streets would become his court before he let that happen.

Dismissing the entire matter from his mind, J-Money rested his arm over his eyes and focused his attention to the problem on the horizon—and that problem was Trey "3B" Bryant. Before J-Money could devise a solution to handle 3B, his phone began to vibrate. He reached over and grabbed it off the nightstand. He stared at the name that involuntarily sat him straight up in the bed. He answered the call. "Yeah … Give me thirty minutes."

J-Money hung up the phone and began to gather his clothes scattered over the floor. If his other two partners wanted to have lunch together, it meant they had a problem that needed to be resolved with a sense of urgency. Salvatore Barozzi of the Barozzi Mafia crime family and Aaron Ullman of Uman records were never in the same place at once. They worked this way to keep the Feds from linking them as business partners.

Nearly half of the drugs on the streets of the United States were supplied by them. They pushed tons of meth, weed, heroin, ecstasy, and cocaine through the record companies that Salvatore, Aaron Ullman, and Herbert Wolff owned. The streets were their kingdom and they controlled it with an iron fist.

"Chloe, I need to bounce. Hit me up later," J-Money said as he slipped on his slacks.

"A'ight," she replied with her attention focused on her smartphone, as she made her way to the bathroom. After finding the number she was looking for, she pressed it. "Mia, it's me … I need you to contact your friend … Yeah."

Chloe hung up the phone and sat it down on the edge of the sink, stepping into the steamy hot shower. Since J-Money was unwilling to make her a widow, she had to take matters into her own hands.

Chapter 8

Thirty minutes later, J-Money walked into the restroom of the popular Italian restaurant, The Factory. Before he headed to the back wall, he checked all the stalls. He wanted to be sure he was alone in here, despite what the guard outside the door said.

He approached the tile on the back wall and pushed in a few squares in what appeared to be a random order. A part of the restroom wall sunk in and slid back, revealing a secret room. This was where they processed the drugs, packaged it, and shipped it out to the streets. Also, the money was brought here to be counted, bagged, and delivered to several banks that cleaned it for them.

The wall slid closed behind J-Money as he strolled over to the table where Aaron Ullman and Salvatore Barozzi were enjoying a drink. He pulled out a chair and joined them.

"Salvatore, you don't have to say it," J-Money began. "I already know Herb is a problem we're about to have."

Tony Steele

Salvatore said nothing, just nodded as he picked up the fifty-year-old brandy and poured J-Money a glass. The Barozzi crime family had been around since the days of Lucky Luciano. The reason they remained one of the most powerful Mafia families in the nation was their ability to fly underneath the Feds' radar. They weren't flamboyant, nor did they display their force. They conducted themselves in the same way as other businessmen in corporate America— when they needed somebody murdered, they did it quietly and subtly.

"I know if there was anybody who would sense this in Herb, it would be you," replied 46-year-old Salvatore, as he crossed his leg over his lap and raked his fingers through his jet black hair. He lacked the typical mobster persona— he had no ruthless attitude, no Italian cocky swagger. His persona fit perfectly with the image the Barozzi family was trying to portray, that of a simple business owner.

Aaron Ullman spoke up. "So Herbert Wolff is a problem we have to deal with right now. My DC friends have informed me that the FBI might be picking him up any day now and charging him with tax invasion." Aaron sat forward, resting his arms on the table. He looked to be a couple years older than Salvatore, and he was just as powerful. He had political ties that reached from DC to Israel, and he had Jewish Mafia connections as well. Aaron and Herbert were both Jewish, and even though they were a part of the same

68

cultural community sworn not to kill their own, Herbert was a problem that could destroy everything they had built.

"We have to make this potential problem go away," J-Money said flatly. Though no one in the room was saying it, Herbert was a situation they wanted him to handle on his own. This part of their partnership—pre-meditated murder—was a lane they stayed clear of and let him deal with.

J-Money didn't have a problem with doing the dirty work. His right hand man, Farook Hall, was good at making people like Herbert Wolff disappear without a trace, never linking anything back to him.

J-Money fanned the glass of brandy underneath his nose and took a sip. "I'll have Farook relieve us of our stress today."

"Then there is nothing else to be said," Salvatore stated.

"I want to discuss another problem we have," Aaron said.

"And that is?" asked Salvatore after taking a sip of his brandy.

"Trey Bryant, otherwise known as 3B."

J-Money had expected the conversation to eventually lead here. 3B had been a thorn in his and Aaron's side since Herbert signed him seven years ago. If 3B wasn't beefing with J-Money's artist, Frankie White, he was burying himself between the thighs of Aaron's niece, Arlene. Her love for 3B got so deep, he had to set 3B up and send him to prison in order to break the hold he had on her.

Now 3B was out and he would be a real threat—a threat J-Money would have to eventually handle.

Salvatore, on the other hand, was in a different position on this one. He loved making money just as much as the next man, and 3B was one of his *biggest* earners. 3B's agent and accountant worked for Salvatore and they made sure he got his share of whatever 3B earned. It was the only reason 3B wasn't somewhere face-down in his own blood. He considered 3B as a loudmouth who didn't know when to shut up. He couldn't stand guys like 3B.

"Don't worry about 3B," said Salvatore. "I'll deal with him. For right now, I need you to focus on this Herbert thing."

J-Money downed the last of his drink and pushed himself to his feet. "Then I best get going."

"And J-Money …" The call of his name stopped him dead in his tracks without a glance over his shoulder. "Call Aaron once the job is done so he can start getting the paperwork in order. We don't need Herbert's record company going to his gold-digging wife."

J-Money replied with a thumb in the air, then looked to the several screens that viewed the entire restroom and even the private stalls. He pressed the red button that triggered the hidden door and waited as the wall went through the process of opening, then he stepped out.

The wall slid closed behind him with a tiny *click*.

Chapter 9

The banging on the door woke Gina Rogers out of her drunken slumber. She was almost certain her assistant, Emily, was the one disturbing her sleep. It would be next to impossible to ignore her. Emily would knock on the door until she got up.

Gina Rogers rolled her legs out of bed and buried her bare feet onto the plush carpet. She drowned her face in her hands as she gathered her senses. She had a long night of drugs, partying, and sex.

"I'm up, Emily. So stop banging on the damn door. Shit!"

"All right then. Start getting yourself ready. You have 3B's welcome home party to go to."

"Okay," Gina said, flopping back onto the bed with a long sigh. She hated 3B with a passion. She and 3B were always arguing about something. A couple times they nearly came to blows, and it was all over the title of a song they were both featured on. They were two people who just couldn't get along for nothing. Herbert threatened to set back the release of her upcoming album just to get her to show up to the party. It was the only reason she was going. She didn't want to be around him at all.

Gina opened the nightstand drawer and pulled out a small mahogany box. This was what she called her "special box." Inside was every drug known to man. Being high on some kind of drug was the only way she would be able resist the urge of punching 3B in the jaw.

She chose some cocaine to start her day off with, dumping the powder onto a handheld mirror on the nightstand. She picked up a piece of a used straw and began to pack her nose with coke. Though she lived the lifestyle of a princess, she was far from one. When she wasn't doing her music thing, she squandered her life away with partying, drugs, and alcohol.

Feeling completely awake now, Gina bounced to her feet and headed to the bathroom for a shower. She peeled off her Victoria's Secret camisole and laced panties, exposing her flawless cinnamon brown skin. She turned on the water and stepped her naked body underneath the warm water, already feeling rejuvenated.

***

Emily took another impatient glance at her watch and continued her pacing outside of Gina's bedroom. Though their friendship spanned back to the third grade, it had been a complex one. Gina's heavy drug use was another added strain to their relationship. She tried to help her kick the habit, but the dope had her. It was starting to become a losing battle.

Gina was using the drugs as a coping mechanism to deal with her Saudi prince who had called off their wedding. Their break-up destroyed her. He was the one man she truly loved. She had been drowning herself in all sorts of drugs to forget that love.

Emily knew if she didn't get Gina some help soon, the Pop Diva would eventually overdose, becoming another entertainer who died at the hands of drugs.

With a long frustrated sigh, Emily approached the door and held up her balled fist to knock when it suddenly opened.

Gina stood in the doorway with her blonde hair pulled into a ponytail and a pair of buggy-eyed Gucci sunglasses. She wore a skintight shirt with "Boss Bitch" printed in bold pink letters, hugging her 34C breasts. This was the look she wanted to give off at 3B's party.

"You aren't planning to wear that, are you?" Emily asked.

"Yeah. I don't have to dress up like I'm going to the awards for a nigga like 3B. Since the nigga is into simple bitches, I thought I should keep it simple," Gina said with the roll of her neck.

"But ... You know what, forget it. Do you want me to call a cab since you're keeping it simple?"

"Call a cab for what? Where is that bum-ass nigga Edgrado?"

"You fired him last night."

"I did? Damn!" Gina stomped her foot. She couldn't drive because her license was revoked. The judge had warned her that he'd sentence her to 90 days in jail if she was caught driving again, let alone while under the influence of the stimulant cocaine.

She cast a look Emily's way, asking with her eyes if Emily was willing.

Emily shook her head no. "I'm not driving, Gina. And you know why."

A horrible car wreck killed Emily's mother—and nearly killed Emily too—so she refused to get behind the wheel of a car. Gina had spent a lot of money on therapy just to get Emily to ride in the back seat. Getting her to drive them there was out of the question.

Suddenly, Gina snapped her fingers, thinking of someone who could get them to the party in style. "Call Kirara. She doesn't live far from here. She can give us a lift."

Kirara was somebody Emily didn't want to bother, especially with something as trivial as giving them a ride. But knowing Gina Rogers as well as she did, the Pop Diva would hound her until she called Kirara, turning her peaceful day into a nightmare.

Emily slipped one of the straps of her bag off her shoulder and dug inside for her smartphone.

***

Kirara nearly poked herself in the eye when her phone suddenly rang, startling her. She placed her contact lenses in her eyes, then scooped up the phone off the dresser. When she saw it was Emily, she wanted to throw the phone in the trash can. Emily wasn't calling her for small talk. Most likely she was calling for the Pop Diva Gina Rogers. Gina wanted her to do something for her. That was the only time Gina ever phoned her.

Kirara was getting tired of it.

She tried to ignore the ringing smartphone but knew she couldn't. She answered it with a long pause. What she wanted to say to Gina Rogers sounded good in her head, but saying it was a different story. She wasn't the type of person to express her thoughts. She kept them bottled up inside.

Eventually she would have to express her opinion. People like Gina, Herbert, and 3B took advantage of her generosity—and it was starting to build up inside her. It might not end well for the person she unleashed her pent-up rage on.

The call of her name snapped Kirara out of her thoughts and brought her attention back to her phone. "Oh, I'm sorry, Emily. What's up?"

"Would you mind coming to pick us up?"

"Sure. Give me a few minutes," Kirara said, even though she wanted to say no.

Chapter 10

"Nathan, I'm pulling up now."

"You're cool, A.B. I have control of the eyes in the sky."

"All right then. I'll see you in five," Almas said, removing his finger from his ear.

Almas's cold, still eyes combed the delivery lot of the Hilton as he slipped the gearshift of his delivery van into park. He drew the 9mm with the silencer from the crease of his back and checked the chamber. There was a live round in the cylinder waiting to claim Herbert Wolff's life. He let the slide go and stuffed the 9mm in his back, then exited the van. He quickly headed toward the door of the dock. His plan was simple—make Herbert Wolff's murder look like a suicide.

But Almas brought his gun just in case. He was unable to do his own re-con on Herbert, so he was essentially walking into the job blind.

***

The young mocha-skinned woman named Dasha hungrily bit down on her bottom lip to muffle her screams of pleasure as Herbert Wolff threw her leg over his shoulder and buried himself deeper into her wet pussy. Though she didn't have the voluptuous figure of his 24-year-old wife Chloe, she still had a deep juicy box. Dasha was well into her thirties, bearing three children, but somehow her pussy was still tight and sweet. This was what Herbert loved about her; it was why he made sure she was a well-pampered mistress.

Herbert felt the tingling sensation bubbling in the pit of his stomach. Knowing he was at the moment of climax he quickened his stroke. He wanted to bury his load deep inside of her. That was another thing he loved about having sex with Dasha—she had her tubes tied. He didn't have to worry about her showing up at his doorstep with a child. He had one child already and had no desire to have another one. That's why he stayed on Chloe about taking her birth control pills. She was the kind of woman who would use a child to rob him of everything. If they divorced right now, she'd leave the marriage with $5 million and what little she came into the marriage with. He made certain to have his lawyer draw up the prenuptial in that fashion.

Herbert froze, his shaft deep within her, as he ejaculated. He let out an exhausted sigh, rolling off of her onto his back. Dasha bounced out of the bed and headed to the bathroom. "I have to go, Herb. I need to pick up my son and take him to the doctor."

"All right. If you could run me some bath water, I'd really appreciate it."

"I gotcha, baby."

"Thanks." Herbert threw his hands over his face and tried to slow his heavy breathing.

***

As Almas strolled toward the service elevator, he spotted a bellhop pulling off his jacket and running into the employee's restroom holding his stomach. *Must've been a bad meal,* Almas thought. He took this opportunity to detour over to the food cart where the bellhop had dropped his jacket. Almas slipped it on. It was a little tight, but no one would notice.

He started wheeling the cart toward the elevator.

***

Dasha leaned in and kissed Herbert passionately, then strutted toward the door. "Call me later," she said over her shoulder.

"I will," Herbert replied as he pulled up his black slacks and threw on a striped shirt.

He walked over to the dresser and began to stuff his pockets with his knick-knacks—wallet, spare change, smartphone—then he dressed his wrist with a Swiss-made Panerai watch. Herbert stood six foot four, had thick salt and pepper hair with a robust physique. He was a 50-year-old man with the look of someone featured on the cover of *Forbes* magazine, someone like the owner of a foreign clothing design company.

But Herbert wasn't a founder of a Fortune 500 company. Instead, he owned one of the biggest record labels in St. Louis—and he was a dope dealer. Along with his business associates, he supplied half of America's streets with drugs. In the line of business he was in, partnerships didn't last long, and some of his partnerships were reaching their peak. He was beginning to sense that one of his partners no longer trusted him. It was apparent what the outcome would be: death. So he had to get them before they moved in on him.

Herbert dug his phone back out of his pocket and searched for a number that could provide the services he needed to put his plan in motion. As soon as he located the number for his daughter, Samantha Wolff, his phone suddenly rang. When he saw it was his lawyer, he quickly answered the call. He had been expecting the call since his lawyer texted him earlier needing to speak with him.

"What's up, Saul?" Herbert asked.

"I've gotten word that the FBI plans to arrest you any day now for tax invasion."

"You think they're using me to get to Salvatore, Aaron, and J-Money?" Herbert asked, needing to know in order to move on them.

"I don't know. That could be a possibility. We won't know until they arrest you."

"Okay then. Call up our bail bondsman for me."

"I will."

"All right then. I want you to keep me posted. I don't want a surprise arrest."

"Sure, Herbert. Talk to you soon."

Herbert hung up the smartphone and selected Samantha's number. She was a financial investor for the criminal underworld. She had ties to some of New York's deeply rooted criminals who could make his business partners disappear. *My lovely daughter Samantha,* he smiled to himself. *She's the perfect shark every dad dreams his daughter will grow up to be.*

After a couple rings, Samantha Wolff's elegant hello snapped Herbert out of his thoughts. "Sammy, it's dad."

"Hey, dad … I can't speak right now. I'm in a meeting at the moment. Can you call me back in a few minutes?"

"Sure, sweetheart. Love you."

"I love you too, dad. Talk to you in a few minutes."

***

Almas stopped the food cart in front of him, stood upright and knocked on the door.

"Who is it?" came Herbert Wolff's voice.

"Room service with your meal, sir."

"Come in."

With an electronic keycard designed by Nathan Branson himself, Almas swiped the card slot and turned the knob. *It opened!* Almas exclaimed in his head. *Nathan, you're a genius!* He strolled into the room with one hand on the food cart, drawing his 9mm with his other hand, then he bumped the door closed with his hip. He crept up to the door leading into the bedroom. He leveled the gun where he expected Herbert Wolff to step into the line of fire.

Herbert Wolff had thrown on a midnight black Etro suit jacket. He strolled out of the bedroom, then stopped suddenly.

"No sudden movement. Hands where I can see them," Almas whispered coldly into Herbert's ear as soon as he crossed the threshold of the bedroom.

"Take it easy, friend."

"Shut up." Almas shoved Herbert toward the living room. He dug the contract for the purchase of Herbert's record label out of his shirt pocket and tossed it onto the coffee table. "Sign it."

"What am I signing?" Herbert asked as he picked up the papers and a pen.

"Just a little business transaction."

As Herbert unfolded the contract and signed his name on several dotted lines, he glanced over the verbiage that said he was signing over ownership of Wolfgang Records. It seemed his business partners were the first to make a move, beating him to the punch.

"There's nothing I can say that will have you switching your gun to those who hired you?" Herbert asked.

"No," Almas replied plainly with his hand held out for the purchase contract.

Herbert signed the last page, folded up the contract and handed it to Almas.

"Now back up to the window with your back to the glass." Almas motioned toward the full length window behind Herbert.

Without any hesitation Herbert backed up to the window, hands in the air.

"Lean against the glass with your hands tucked deep in the front of your pants."

A heavy sigh escaped Herbert's tightly pressed lips as he did what he was told. His body seemed to weigh more than it appeared as he leaned his back against the window. He swore he could hear the glass begin to crack.

Almas glanced over the three pages to make sure Herbert had dotted his i's and crossed his t's. Seeing everything in order, he fired two shots at the window without looking up from the purchase contract.

The glass shattered and snatched Herbert out of the window as if by some unseen force.

By the time Herbert had his hands out of his pants, the window frame was out of his reach. He was falling to his death too fast to even utter a word. When he finally let out a squeal, it was too late—the ground had come up on him quick; he hit concrete with the same sound as a watermelon being dropped out of the window.

He was dead.

Almas stuffed the 9mm into his back and headed out of the suite. He heard people screaming on the street below just before he shut the door behind him.

***

Farook Hall stepped off the elevator pushing a laundry cart. He was the size of a defensive linebacker. He had the speed and skillset as one also. It was the reason J-Money had no worries that he would succeed at his job. Murder was an art he had perfected. Once unleashed, Farook wouldn't stop until he had killed his mark.

Farook eased his hand into his jacket and took hold of the handle of the .40 Glock in the holster under his arm. He approached suite 1133 and slid the keycard into the lock slot. Before he had a chance to fully enter the room, he knew something was definitely wrong.

A gust of wind greeted him as he stepped in. He didn't need to stick around to know someone had beat him to the job. He backed out of the suite just as quietly as he had entered.

Chapter 11

Nita Candy, who had been 3B's girlfriend since middle school, tried to catch 3B's eye to see what he was thinking, but he never looked her way. He just stared out the window at the scenery floating by. She wanted to know why he hadn't said word since they left the prison. He hadn't even tried to fuck her. She would've at least thought he would be more interested in making love to her than sight-seeing. By the way he was distancing himself, she wondered if the person they were going to see was another woman. If it was, she hoped he made his peace with God, because she wouldn't hesitate to kill him.

The Hummer's privacy window slid down. The driver, Slip, said, "We're here, 3B."

"Thanks, man." Trey Bryant opened the door. "Listen, Slip, get Nita to the party. I'll meet yall there."

"What—" Before Nita could get the rest of the words out of her mouth, Trey leaned over and kissed her.

When he pulled his lips from hers, she let out a breathless sigh. She sunk back in the leather seats, hungrily licking her lips. This was the only way she would remain calm. He didn't need her insisting on going inside with him. She would've lost it once she saw he was here to see another woman. Then he'd be back in prison for putting his hands on her. Because there was no way she wouldn't hesitate to slap him across the face once she saw Safiya Cody. Nita was that kind of female.

Trey hopped out of the Hummer and slammed the door closed before Nita had a chance to snap out of her blissful moment. Neatly straightening out his Hugo Boss sports jacket, he strolled into the White Water nursing home.

"Excuse me, miss. Could you tell me if Safiya Cody is here?" Trey asked as he walked up to the receptionist's desk, lifting the Gucci sunglasses onto the top of his head.

The woman stared up at him. "Yes. I'll page her. May I ask who you are?"

"A family friend. Trey Bryant."

The receptionist picked up the receiver and called Safiya's pager.

Trey flipped his sunglasses down over his eyes and turned away from the woman's gaze. He could see she was trying to place his face. The last thing he wanted was the woman recognizing who he was. He didn't want the nursing home to be swamped with paparazzi. The national media had no idea he was out of prison—yet. That was how he wanted to keep it. He needed to do this for Stanley. He didn't want the world's eyes on him while he carried out his promise.

He had his publicist and lawyer put out a false report of his release date. He knew they would be right on the parking lot when he walked out of prison. He wanted to keep a low profile until he was ready to let the world know he was free.

"Excuse me, Mr. Bryant, Safiya will be out in a minute. You can have a seat," the receptionist said with her arm extending toward the sitting area.

Trey strolled over and took a seat.

The receptionist spoke again. "Mr. Bryant, if I may ask … You aren't by chance the rapper 3B?"

"Nah, I'm not him. His name is Travon Bryant and mine is Trey Bryant," he replied.

"I knew it was silly to ask. Sorry."

"Oh, it's no problem. I get that a lot."

The receptionist stared at him, still debating with herself whether or not he was the famous rapper. After a moment, she looked away.

As Trey relaxed back in the plaid chair, a woman wearing a navy blue nursing uniform strutted down the hallway that led straight toward him. The outfit hugged her shapely figure like a glove. She was an average looking woman with dark brown skin. He couldn't tell if work made her look plain or if it was just natural. Whatever it was, his interest was piqued. This was the kind of woman he liked. Plain Jane. She was a working woman. She earned her living the honest way.

"Mr. Bryant?" asked Safiya Cody with her hand held out.

"Yes." Trey shook her hand. "I came here to give you this."

He reached inside of his jacket, pulling out a letter. He handed to her. She rolled the blank envelope in her hands, searching for some indication of who it was from. She wondered if it was a message from her father but immediately dismissed the idea. The last time he tried to contact her, she had called the institution where he was serving his time and threatened to sue the Department of Corrections if they allowed him to send another letter to her again. To avoid a lawsuit, the administration promised her they would censor all of his outgoing mail. That was three years ago. She hadn't received a letter from her father since.

Curiosity got the better of her and she opened the envelope, pulling out the letter inside. She was expecting something to jump out at her, as she slowly unfolded it and began reading. Her brown eyes managed to roam over only two lines before suddenly going dark. She balled up the letter and tossed it to the floor. Lately, she had been fighting with herself to stay hating her father. The harder she tried, the more she wanted a relationship with him.

It wasn't just her who wanted a relationship with him. Her 8-year-old son was starting to ask about his grandfather. The letter she just received only added more conflict to her decision.

Safiya turned and walked away when Trey grabbed her by the arm. She spun around with a look in her eyes that caused him to release his grip.

"I'm sorry," said Trey. "I didn't mean any harm. I was just fulfilling a promise I made."

"A promise?"

"Yeah." Trey took Safiya by the hand this time and walked her to the back of the waiting area so he could speak to her in private. "I was released from prison today. While I was inside, your dad helped me get my life together. That's why I'm here—to convince you to give him a chance."

Looking into Trey's face, Safiya no longer saw her father as the man whose misdeeds resulted in her mother's death. She was beginning to see him as a man who was trying to redeem himself. The effort her father was taking to change his life, she felt she should give him a chance to reconnect with him. Plus, it would be good for her son since he was getting up in age. Her son needed a man in his life with his own father being absent.

Just thinking about it got her choked up. She cleared her throat, hoping Trey didn't hear how emotional this news had her. "I'll give him a chance," she said.

"Good. Now there's something else he wants you to have."

Safiya arched an eyebrow. "What?"

"Do you have a car?"

"Yeah."

"Okay." Trey glanced at his Cartier watch. He had less than an hour before Nita came looking for him, so they needed to get a move on it. "Can you leave right now?"

"Well, my shift is about to be over in a few minutes."

"Cool. I need you to go clock out right now so we can go. I'll explain everything to you on the way."

"On the way where?"

"As I said before, I'll explain on the way there. For now, just go clock out."

"Okay." Safiya slowly backed away, trying to figure out what was going on. She headed off down the hallway.

By the way the receptionist looked at Trey, he could tell she wasn't buying his lie any longer. She was calling over nurses to her desk to confirm who he really was. He turned his back to her and took another glance at his watch. He had to get out of here. He didn't need the mass hysteria of a celebrity sighting.

Suddenly, his phone began to ring, startling him out of his thoughts. He dug his phone out of the inside pocket of his sports jacket and stared at the number. His jaws tightened when he saw it was Nita. He wanted to send the call to voicemail, but decided against it, taking a long pause before he answered it.

"What's up, Nita?"

"Where are you?" she asked, a little agitated.

Trey's knuckles cracked under the pressure of his tightly balled fist. Nita had no right to question him about his whereabouts. She had lost that privilege with the betrayal she committed while he was in prison.

He wanted to tell her off, let her know he knew all about her little dirty secret. Instead, he held his tongue. He would make Nita fess up in due time. For right now he needed to keep his mind focused on upholding his promise to Stanley.

"Listen, Nita. I'll call you when I finish handling my business. So let me get back to it and stop calling me ..." Trey pressed the end button, then stuffed the phone back in his pocket. He knew he would pay later for hanging up on her. But it felt good, no matter what she had in store for him.

Chapter 12

Other than needing a fresh coat of paint, the house Safiya parked in front of didn't look too bad, especially after sitting abandoned for the last twenty-five years. This residence had once been Stanley's money house. This was where he counted up his earnings. Before he killed his best friend, he buried a million dollars for his daughter. Since she refused to speak to him, the money stayed buried.

Until now.

Safiya had amassed a ton of debt due to her son's father's excessive spending and bad investments. He had her three hundred and fifty thousand dollars in debt to several lenders because of his failed businesses. She had to do double and triple shits to relieve some of the pressure of the debt she was in.

What Trey had told her about the buried cash, Safiya found it hard to believe. She knew her father was using her situation just to reconnect with her. She immediately dismissed the thought. She couldn't grasp the idea that her father would stoop so low, lying about buried money to get a response from her. She had to wait and see before she'd think otherwise.

"You ready?" Trey asked as he opened the passenger side door.

Safiya exhaled a slow breath, calming herself down. "Yeah."

Trey reached into the back seat and grabbed the pickax and shovel he had her buy at a hardware store, then he rose from the gray seats of the minivan. He slung the tools over his shoulder and started up the walkway. He had his lawyer purchase the house from the family of Stanley's right hand man a couple months ago, a man that was now dead due to prostate cancer.

"Do you really believe what my father told you?" Safiya asked.

Trey didn't know how to answer. He wanted to believe what Stanley told him about the money, but a part of him was skeptical. He decided to keep his doubts to himself. "Yes," he said, "I believe what Stanley told me."

"Okay then. So will I."

Trey slid the key into the lock and opened the door.

The stale air of the uninhabited house greeted them. Trey fanned the cloud of dust that the opening door had stirred. They stepped inside.

"So where is this money supposed to be hidden at?" Safiya asked.

"The basement. Come on."

Since the house was one story, the door to the basement was most likely in the kitchen. That was where Safiya and Trey headed.

Having his lawyer pay off the electric bill was the best thing Trey could have done, he thought, as he opened the door to the basement. The stairway was pitch black. He couldn't see anything past the threshold.

He flicked on the switch beside the door. The basement instantly lit up with an audible humming. He held out his hand, which Safiya grabbed without hesitation. He led her down the wooden stairs, each step creaking under their combined weight.

The way Stanley explained it to him, the money was buried under a red dot on the back wall. He searched the wall but didn't find the mark. He immediately became concerned and wondered if he had answered Safiya's question about belief too hastily.

The need for what Stanley told him to be true continued to push Trey forward. That was when he saw it: a faded red dot a couple feet from the floor, the size of a silver dollar. He would've missed it if he hadn't been looking as hard as he was.

"There's the mark, Safiya," Trey said as he peeled off his jacket and shirt, then handed them to Safiya.

The way the white tanktop he wore hugged his well-chiseled body, Safiya found herself involuntarily reaching for a touch. His body had so much definition to it that his muscles seemed to appear unreal. She had to feel him to convince herself he was human.

"Stand back, Safiya."

She embarrassingly snatched back her outreached hand, as she took a couple steps back.

Inhaling a couple deep breaths, Trey swung the pickax with all his might. The concrete shattered into pieces. He grabbed the shovel and began to scoop away the chunks of concrete until he uncovered the soil. He let out a grunt and started to dig.

After ten minutes of clearing away the dirt, Trey hit something. He was so excited that his cheeks began to burn as he shoveled away the last of the dirt, unearthing a metal box no more than three feet long. He squatted down and pulled the box out of its resting place. He popped the latches and drew back the lid.

"Holy shit," was all Safiya could say as her eyes were greeted by bundles of tens, twenties, fifties, and hundred dollar bills tightly wrapped in plastic, stuffed inside of the metal box.

"I guess your father was telling the truth," said Trey, all smiles.

"I guess so," Safiya replied in disbelief, as she handed Trey's shirt and jacket to him. She dropped to her knees in front of the money.

Trey was slipping on his shirt when his smartphone began to ring. He fetched his phone and stared at the screen. It was exactly who he assumed it would be calling him sooner or later. Nita Candy. He had to get his heavy breathing under control. He didn't want Nita to think he was having sex and go berserk.

Once his breath came back, he answered the call. "What's up, Nita? … Yeah, I'm on my way now … A'ight. Bye … Love you too." Trey hung up the phone and stuffed it back into his jacket pocket. "I hate to run out on you like this, but I need to bounce."

"Okay," she said. "Are you gonna take your half of the money now?"

Trey's forehead wrinkled. "None of it is mines. Your father wanted you to have it all."

"I can't take all of this. You deserve half."

"Just pay me back by staying in contact with your father. Can you do that for me?"

She blinked, fighting back tears. Then she gave him a warm hug. "Thank you."

"You're welcome, Safiya."

"Do you need me to drop you off somewhere?"

"Nah. I'm good. I'll call my nigga to have him come pick me up." Trey eased the sports jacket over his broad shoulders and gave it a firm tug, straightening it out. "If you need anything, all you gotta do is call."

"I will. And thanks again."

"Do you need me to help you get this to your car?"

"No. I can handle it. You've already done enough for me as it is."

"It was not a problem. Just helping out a friend. You take it easy, okay?"

"I will. And you do the same."

Trey gave her a thumbs up, then jogged up the steps, leaving Safiya alone with her trust fund.

Chapter 13

Nervously, Mr. Walter Fisher twiddled his thumbs as his narrowed eyes swept over the dimly lit underground garage. He was a slender-built reporter for a local tabloid paper, *Scoop News*, that featured today's hottest celebrities. It wasn't the lifestyle of the stars that earned him a Pulitzer Prize; it was the secrets the entertainment business kept hidden from the public. This time he uncovered a secret that could turn into a life or death situation.

One of his insiders gave him the scoop on Gatz Records and its founder and CEO, J-Money. It seemed most of the drugs sold on the corners of St. Louis and nearly all of the Midwest were supplied by J-Money and his associates, Salvatore Barozzi, Herbert Wolff, and Aaron Ullman. They were deadly men. He had to tread lightly. The person he was in this garage to meet had information that would expose their entire criminal operation.

"I kind of figured it was you," said a heavy voice from the shadows. "If there was anybody with a knack for sticking his nose where it doesn't belong, it's you."

The color drained from Walter's face as he searched wildly for the face to the voice. Since this wasn't the person he was here to meet, he wondered, *Did J-Money learn that I was poking into Gatz Records' income?* If this was the case, the person who just spoke to him was most likely his executioner. He had to get out of here!

He took a step back toward his car, which was a few feet away.

"It's pointless to run, Mr. Walter Fisher."

His name being mentioned by the stranger froze him in place. He had to think of a way out of this or he was as good as dead.

Walter wet his lips as he thought of the perfect pitch to sell, his last chance to save his own life. "You don't want to do this, sir. If you give me your story—if you tell me all you know about J-Money—I'll pay you double what I was going to pay my informant."

Several shots rang out. Walter felt something massive push him to the cold concrete with a loud thump. He lifted his head just enough to see that his chest was leaking blood from at least four bullet holes. Another shot rang out, striking him in the forehead. He lay dead, blood pooling out from underneath him.

A man in a cheap suit stepped from the shadows. He tossed the murder weapon near Walter's body and pulled out a prepaid cell phone. The number he wanted was already on the screen. He pressed it, then brought the phone up to his ear. "It's me, Quentin ... Yeah. Mr. Fisher is no longer a problem." He hung up the cell phone and headed to his car.

***

J-Money stuffed his phone into his pocket and took a sip of his glass of brandy. His hardened gaze cut back to the full-length window that offered a beautiful scene of the St. Louis Gateway Arch, a 630-foot symbol of westward expansion. Walter Fisher could have been a big problem. It was why he had Detective Quentin Bosco handle Walter. With Quentin being a cop, he was the perfect person to get rid of Walter without it linking back to J-Money.

J-Money knew Detective Bosco when he was in the streets. He and Bosco had an arrangement worked out. Bosco provided him with the names of dealers, and J-Money would rob them. They split the take 50/50. When J-Money got into the rap game, he hired the detective for security detail and for jobs that Farook Hall couldn't carry out.

The sound of approaching footsteps shook J-Money out of his thoughts. He downed the remainder of his drink and turned to his unexpected guest.

Farook walked in. He hiked up his slacks and eased down on the Russian-leather sofa, folding his leg over his lap. "We have a situation."

"That is?" J-Money asked, as he sat down into a matching arm chair.

"It seems our friend, Herbert Wolff, has committed suicide."

J-Money looked curious. "Herbert has saved us the trouble of killing him?"

"His suicide might not be the solution to our predicament."

"Why do you say that?"

"Because I think he was killed. If that is so, it means someone is trying to muscle in on our business."

What Farook said made sense. Herbert didn't seem like the type to kill himself. Salvatore and Aaron wouldn't want to hear this news. A war was something neither of them wanted. But it was one they might not be able to avoid.

"I need you to turn over every stone you can to find out who was behind Herbert's death," said J-Money.

Farook pushed himself to his feet. "Okay. Do you want whoever is responsible to be dealt with?"

"No. Let's see how it plays out first before we make any moves. And as soon as possible, take care of our friend Detective Bosco."

***

Claire Collins, a senior reporter for the *Scoop News*, sat at her desk typing on her laptop. She looked up when she saw her secretary Selena standing in the doorway. The young woman looked like she was holding in some great burden. "Yes, Selena?"

"I just received a call that Walter was murdered earlier tonight."

Selena's words shoved Claire back in her chair. Walter had told her to meet him for drinks later to discuss a big story he was working on. Now he was dead. She couldn't grasp the thought that this big story he kept secret resulted in his death. He had survived several attempts on his life without suffering a scratch. She had to find out what was going on.

Claire grabbed her purse and cell phone and bounced to her feet. "Send all my calls to my phone," she said, strutting toward the door.

"Okay. What are you going to do?"

"Find out what the hell happened to my friend."

Chapter 14

The thrill of being home had Trey's palms sweaty, as he fanned them dry. Wolfgang Records wasn't the typical 'hood record company. It was as classy as some of the big-name record labels with state of the art recording equipment, top of the line security and accommodations that made the place more of a five-star hotel than a record label.

This was where Trey felt the most at home. He couldn't wait to get in the booth and start putting down tracks.

If there was anything he missed the most while being incarcerated, it was the booth. Many nights he laid up in his bunk thinking about being in the studio while he filled his notebook with impassioned lyrics. Now his chance was here, and he couldn't wait to unleash it on the microphone. The mere thought made his skin tingle.

The bright fluorescent lights of the sign bearing the Wolfgang Records logo of a wolf howling brought him out of his thoughts. He let out a nervous breath, then climbed out of the Hummer.

He walked up to the building and pushed through the double doors.

Nita, who was standing off by herself pouting, forced a smile when she saw Trey Bryant walk inside. She was about to ask him where he had been when a band of guests swarmed ahead of her. She leaned against the wall and waited until he had a moment to himself. She knew he was with another woman and wanted to hear the lie he would give her. She had warned him she would no longer tolerate his constant cheating once he got out of prison. She refused to let him put her through that heartache again.

"Charlie Hustle, what's up baby boy?" said Trey, greeting his old friend with a firm handshake. "You ready to get this paper?"

"No doubt, 3B."

A young man wearing a pair of snug designer jeans and a white St. Louis Cardinals jersey with matching cap approached Trey. His name was Philip Bowie, aka Phibo. He was an up-and-coming artist. Herbert signed him just before Trey went to prison. Phibo was one of the many rappers he couldn't wait to get into the studio with.

"What's good, Phibo?" said Trey with a smile. He gave the youngster dap.

"Shit," Phibo replied, smiling back. "Just waiting for you to get home so we can take over the game."

"That's what I'm saying, my nigga."

Trey caught sight of Gina Rogers. She was another artist he needed on his upcoming album. She had the perfect voice for the chorus to a single he planned to drop in a couple days. "Listen, Phibo, I need you in the studio tomorrow morning."

"I'm there, my man."

"A'ight. I'll see you in the a.m." Trey gave Phibo a pat on the back, then made his way over to where Gina Rogers stood talking with Emily, her assistant.

Coldly, Gina Rogers stared at 3B working his way toward her as she downed her third glass of Dom Perignon. She tried her best to maintain her anger the closer 3B approached. She wished she had more drugs in her system right now. It was the only way she could deal with him.

Emily didn't need to ask Gina what was bothering her. She knew what it was when she saw 3B heading in their direction. She had to calm Gina down. She wanted to enjoy the evening and not spend it sitting in the holding tank at the Justice Center. She needed some dick and hoped 3B would be the man to satisfy her craving.

"Gina, can we please have a peaceful evening without finding ourselves in jail?"

Gina looked at Emily with a glare that would have normally made Emily take a step back, but this time Gina got no reaction out of her. Emily threw a glare back.

"You won't have any problem out of me tonight," Gina said. "Now, get me a drink." She held the empty champagne glass out to Emily.

Emily snatched the glass from Gina Rogers's hand. "I am warning you. If you mess this night up for me, I'm through fucking with you."

"I told you I'll chill. Now get my drink," Gina Rogers replied, shooing Emily off.

Emily grunted and headed over to the waiter handing out drinks.

"Miss Gina Rogers," said Trey, as he approached, "if there is anybody I'm dying to work with, it is you."

What 3B said caused Gina Rogers to take a step back. She couldn't tell if he was serious or not. She leaned in to be certain she had heard him right.

"Listen, I got this hook on a song you would be perfect for. So what's up, you interested?"

"Umm ..."

"Yeah. She would love to do a song with you, 3B," Emily said as she walked up. She handed Gina her drink.

"Cool. I'll meet you here at ten," said Trey.

"Okay," Gina finally managed to utter, coming out of her shock.

"I'll get with you later. I still have rounds to make," said Trey, waving goodbye.

"Can you believe 3B wanted to do a song with you?!" Emily exclaimed.

"Nah," Gina replied snidely, taking a sip of her champagne. As long as she had been signed to Wolfgang Records, 3B had never asked her to do a song with him. Honestly, he had never cut a track with anybody on the label. He always did songs with artists from other record labels. She wondered if this change in him was due to his incarceration.

Whatever the case may be, she was glad he decided to be a team player.

Still standing by herself, Nita Candy was tired of waiting for 3B to come to her. She could see she had to go to him if she wanted to get the answer for his whereabouts earlier. She was willing to stake her life on it that 3B was having a private welcoming home party between some bitch's thighs.

She gulped down half of her glass of Bollinger and strutted over to where 3B was talking with several of the label's producers, when her phone began to ring. She dug into her cherry red Fendi lambskin bag, praying it wasn't another text from the same person who had been trying to reach her since dropping 3B off at the nursing home earlier. If it was him texting her, then she was in deep shit. She couldn't accuse 3B of cheating when she had been the unfaithful one. It wasn't just a recent thing either. This had been going on since 3B had went to prison.

Nita stared at the number. It was, to her dismay, Taveras "Getty-Gat" Morris texting her, in need of some sex. He was an artist under J-Money's label, Gatz Records.

"Listen, babe. I'm going to step into the studio for a second, then we can bounce to get the real party started," Trey said as he walked up.

Nita nearly jumped out of her skin, stuffing her phone in her bag. "Sure, I'm ready to go anyway."

"You a'ight?" he asked, eyeing Nita suspiciously.

"Yeah. You just startled me. Go ahead, so we can get out of here. I got a negligee I'm dying to show off." She stared him directly in the eyes, flashing an innocent smile.

"Negligee, for what? You won't have it on long enough for me to admire it." Trey kissed her on the cheek.

"Boy, you're crazy. Now go." Nita shoved him toward the door.

Playfully, he staggered away, then headed for the door.

Once her man was out of her sight, Nita dug in her bag and continued to locate Getty-Gat's number. It seemed like he wasn't getting the message, so he had to hear it from her lips that they were over.

She stepped off to the side and called him. "Getty-Gat, stop calling me. I told you we're over."

"I'm not trying to hear that, girl."

"Since you ain't getting the picture, I'll make it clearer for you. We're over, so stop calling me!"

"I don't believe you. The only way I'll believe you is if you say it to my face."

There was a long pause. Getty-Gat knew Nita was trying to psych herself up to tell him no. But she could never tell him no. She would come, and he would have her telling him yes many times over.

Nita didn't want to give in to him. She had to stand her ground. She tried to force the right response from her lips, but instead she ended up saying, "Okay. I'll be there in an hour."

***

Emily spotted 3B heading for the door. She knew he was on his way to the studio. This was her chance to have him put out the fire between her legs. It was right before he went to prison when he and Gina Rogers were on tour. They had been partying at New York's hottest nightclub, Club Inferno, after one of his concerts. Gina Rogers decided to move the party to her suite once the club had closed. It didn't take long for the party to turn into a "Gina Party"—sex, drugs, and alcohol. When Gina began to party in that manner, she'd eventually pass out on the couch. Emily would always help her into bed. But that time, after she tucked Gina in, Emily wandered over to 3B's presidential suite.

Emily didn't know if it was the Kush he was smoking on or just his natural swagger that made him so intoxicating, but she couldn't help herself when she was around him— especially in private. Before she realized it, she was in his bed with him, and he was burying himself deep between her thighs.

Emily wanted that good fuck again. She hadn't met another man who could satisfy her the way 3B did the night they made love until the sun rose over Times Square.

"I need to use the restroom," Emily said to Gina, handing over the glass of Dom Perignon she had hardly tasted.

"A'ight," said Gina.

Emily quickly headed toward the door as Gina Rogers shrugged her shoulders and downed the rest of Emily's drink.

***

Trey Bryant eased into the leather seat in front of the most expensive mixing board in the industry. This was where he would resurrect his career and put himself back on top of the rap game again.

"Why are you playing me off as if you don't know me? What you mad at me for?" Emily asked seductively.

A heavy sigh escaped Trey's tightly pressed lips. Emily was a woman he didn't want to see. Since their sexual encounter in New York, he couldn't get her out of his mind. He even found himself masturbating in the prison shower or laying up in his bunk fantasizing about her all night.

Trey bounced to his feet and closed the gap between them, backing her up against the wall. Heat rolled from beneath Emily's skirt against his legs. She wanted this to happen as badly as he did.

"What about your woman?" Emily asked with a long horny moan, letting every syllable roll off her tongue seductively.

"Fuck her."

Trey twirled Emily around and planted her face first against the wall. He pulled up her skintight dress and eased her lace panties down over her wide hips. He hungrily groped her soft butt cheeks. He had never met a woman with ass cheeks as soft as hers. It was like squeezing a fluffy pillow.

He unbuttoned his slacks, dropped his boxers and slid his dick between the lips of her hot, wet pussy.

Emily bit down on her bottom lip as she let out a low moan. "*Ummm!* Now that's what mama *neeeeds*. Make this pussy purr."

She felt every inch of his dick as he buried himself deep inside of her. He was hung like a porn star and he knew how to use it like one. She had been dying for him to fuck her. He was one of the few men who could make her cum.

"Oh shit! This pussy is so good, damn!" Trey moaned with his mouth caked with her saliva.

"And it's all yours. Beat it up."

"That's exactly what I'm gonna do," he whispered in her ear.

Emily rolled her hips with his strokes. Trey felt that manly sensation building in the pit of his stomach as he quickened his thrusts.

"Ew, baby. Make this pussy cum." Emily slipped a leg out of her panties and spread her legs farther apart so he could get deeper inside of her.

"Oh shit. I'm about to bust," Trey grunted.

"Fill me up with your cum."

"Here I come, baby."

"Trey!" they heard Nita call out to him.

"Fuck!" Trey uttered under his breath, and at the same time he came inside of Emily. He pulled out of her and yanked up his slacks. "Go into the booth," he said, pointing to a door in the middle of the room.

Emily snatched down her dress, scooped up her panties and ducked off into the booth.

Trey dropped into the swivel chair and pretended to mess around with the mixer as the entrance door opened. He spun around toward Nita. "What's up, babe?"

"I gotta go. My mom just hit me saying she needs to see me. Something about an emergency." Nita leaned in and kissed him passionately. "I'll meet you at home."

"Okay." Trey kissed her again and turned back to the mixer.

Nita fished her phone out of her bag as she quickly strutted toward the door when she bumped into someone. She looked up into the Italian man's face briefly, more interested in the text she was about to send to Getty-Gat. "Sorry," she said absentmindedly as she stepped around and strolled out of the studio.

The Italian man greeted Trey with a smile. "3B, it's good to see you free."

"That ain't who I think it is, is it?" Trey said, rising to his feet and embracing the Mafia boss Salvatore Barozzi. He was the one who introduced him to Herbert Wolff. Salvatore had overheard him battle-rapping at his club one night and convinced Herbert that Trey was a superstar in the making.

"Yeah, it's me in the flesh," Salvatore said.

"Please sit."

"I'm cool. I'm not going to be long. I just came to talk to you about something now that you're out."

Trey slumped down in the chair and cuffed his hands behind his head. "What's up?"

"Well ..." Salvatore's ringing cell phone cut him off. He reached into his suit jacket. "Excuse me. I need to take this," he said when he saw it was J-Money calling him. He stepped away, knowing J-Money was calling to confirm that Herbert had been killed. "Hello? ... Yeah ... Yeah? ... When? ... Okay. I'll see you there."

"What's going on, Salvatore?" Trey asked, concerned.

Salvatore hung up his phone as he turned to Trey. "It seems your boss, Herbert Wolff, committed suicide earlier today."

"What?" Trey jumped to his feet.

"Yeah. I gotta go and see what the hell is going on. I'll talk to you tomorrow."

"A'ight."

Salvatore stuffed his phone back into his pocket and headed out of the studio.

The door to the booth opened and Emily walked out in tears. "Is what he said true?"

"I don't know," said Trey, "but let's go find out."

Trey took Emily by the arm and walked her out of the studio.

Chapter 15

The moonlit sky reflected off the pond water, giving the scenery a romantic setting, as Chloe Wolff strolled onto the terrace. She sipped on a glass of red wine. The breathtaking sight was one of many in this mansion, but this view she truly delighted in.

Herbert had built this mega home from the ground up. The mere thought of Herbert began to stir all kinds of emotions up inside of her, mostly feelings of relief and excitement. She received the news of his death earlier today—and it really made her love the place even more, because it was hers now, *all hers!* She also inherited $300 million dollars and Wolfgang Records. If there was anything she wanted more than the mansion and the money, it had to be Wolfgang Records. She had always dreamed of owning a record label but didn't want to start from the bottom.

Now, she owned one—a well-established one at that, with some of today's hottest artists. All she had to do now was sit back, churn out chart-topping hits and take over the music industry.

"Thank you, Herbert. May your miserable ass rest in peace," Chloe said, looking toward the night sky, pouring out her glass of red wine.

The sudden ring of the doorbell drew Chloe's eyes from the sky toward the bedroom. She wondered who could be visiting her in her hour of mourning. She strolled inside to greet her unannounced guest.

***

The old silver-haired butler opened the door and, with an arched eyebrow, stared at the clean-cut man standing in front of him. "May I help you, sir?"

"Yeah. Is Chloe home?" J-Money asked.

"Yes, sir. Please come in."

J-Money popped the two buttons loose of his gray Vince Camuto suit jacket and entered the mansion. This was the first time he had visited Herbert's house, and he was impressed. Cream-colored marble tile laced the floor. A Renaissance staircase curved to the second floor, where Chloe exited a pair of mahogany doors he assumed led to the master bedroom.

"Gregory, you can leave us," Chloe said to her butler, as she strutted down the staircase.

"Yes, madam." Gregory bowed slightly and strolled off toward the kitchen.

"Please." Chloe extended her arm toward the living room.

J-Money stuffed his hands in his pockets and entered the living room, taking a seat on the sofa.

"Would you like a drink?" Chloe asked over her shoulder as she approached the wet bar.

"No. I'm good."

Chloe poured herself a glass of Herbert's 100-year-old scotch. "What do I owe the pleasure of this unexpected visit?"

"We have a problem." J-Money spread open his suit jacket and folded his leg over his lap.

"And that is?"

"I have concerns with what happened to your husband, especially with you asking me to kill him." J-Money waited to see her reaction.

Chloe looked confused. "Why would you say that? My husband committed suicide."

"Just curious." J-Money rose to his feet. "There's something I must attend to. I'll call you tomorrow."

"Where do you think you're going? You came all the way over here to accuse me of killing my husband, and then you're gonna leave?"

"I didn't accuse you of anything."

Chloe swayed over to J-Money, amused by his accusation. She adjusted the lapels of his jacket. "I need a shoulder to cry on."

He smiled. "Then my shoulder is yours."

"Follow me then," Chloe said as she backed away, curling her finger for him to follow.

Chapter 16

Getty-Gat had converted the once four-family flat into a mini mansion. The most expensive marble, hardwood flooring, carpet, furniture, and appliances decked the place out. If the apartment building hadn't been in the heart of the ghetto, a real estate agent could easily get a million and a half for it, easy.

No matter how much money Getty-Gat had put into the apartment building, no matter how many purchase offers he got, he still wouldn't sell it. This was his home. It was where he grew up, with his mother, until a couple years ago when breast cancer claimed her life.

After pouring his second glass of Hennessy Paradis, Getty-Gat walked over to the sofa where his light-skinned beauty Ava rolled up a cigarillo of Cookie Kush. He flopped down onto the soft leather cushion and took a sip of his drink. He glanced around his home and nodded his head, impressed with himself. It always amazed him how his hustle game had him living like a king. He made millions in the rap and dope game. He had several trap houses throughout St. Louis, bringing in major cash.

A sudden knock at the door drew his attention out of his thoughts.

"Get the door, Ava."

Ava rose to her feet and headed out of the living room.

Getty-Gat groped his erection as he stared at Ava's butt bouncing uncontrollably in her boy shorts. She was his "mean woman" and his partner in crime. She oversaw his clique of women, hustlers he named the Trapping Honeys.

Ava entered the living room accompanied by Nita Candy.

A sly smirk slid across Getty's lips as he stared at Nita stepping in front of him. It wasn't her looks or sex game that made him want to keep up their relationship; he had countless women who looked finer than her and were masters in the art of sex. He kept Nita around because of her man, Trey "3B" Bryant.

Before the rap game, Trey and Getty ran the streets of St. Louis as rivals. They traded gunfire more than once, one time in the middle of the day on Natural Bridge Road. Their feud spread over into dis records, more shoot-outs, and club fights. Frankie White, who was signed to the same label as Getty, shared the same hatred for 3B and wanted 3B dead.

But Getty felt the best way to handle 3B was stealing his girl from him.

Getty-Gat was a boss, so he carried and conducted business like one. Stealing 3B's girl from him was the classiest thing a boss could do to a man, next to giving the order to have him killed.

"Would you like a drink?" Getty asked Nita, staring at her enticingly. He took a sip of his drink.

Nita looked away, trying not to make eye contact. She knew if their eyes met for too long, she wouldn't be able to resist him. He sparked a sexual fire in her that could only be extinguished by him.

"No drink," she said. "I'm good."

"So what is it that you gotta tell me?"

"It's over between us," Nita said sassily.

Ava propped her legs up on the coffee table so far apart that her pussy, dampened with moisture through her boy shorts, was fully exposed. "Oh, come on, Nita. Don't leave us," she said. "I like having you around."

"Like I said—" Nita's next words fell off her lips as she caught sight of Ava's pussy. She couldn't keep her sexual hunger in check any longer.

She lost it.

Her pussy constricted against her will, then a warm sensation of cum trickled down her inner thigh. This was the reason why she was calling it off with Getty-Gat. He had her doing things she would've never done otherwise. Having sex with a woman … Nita would have never done that if it wasn't for him. He brought out her deepest, vilest desires—and one of them was Ava. Nita loved eating Ava's pussy. It tasted like sweet, organic strawberries. Her favorite.

Ava caught Nita staring and slowly pulled off her boy shorts, then spread her legs farther apart, causing the velvety lips of her pussy to bloom open. "Oh, look what I've gone and done," said Ava, innocently. "How silly of me."

Nita licked her lips as her sexual appetite took over her body. She had to taste Ava—right now. She dropped her Fendi bag to the floor and walked over to Ava as if she was in a trance.

"You want a taste?" Ava asked as she slid her hand downward to her center.

Nita nodded her head.

"Then quench your thirst." Ava propped herself up against the arm of the sofa as Nita approached her. She helped Nita out of her dress and panties and then lowered Nita's head between her legs.

Nita threw Ava's legs over her shoulders so she could bury her mouth deep into Ava's meaty nectar.

"Mmm. Give me what I need," Ava hissed through gritted teeth.

A loud moan escaped Nita's mouth as Getty-Gat entered her from behind. She immediately started to cum, and as soon as Getty-Gat felt her juices sliding down his balls, he pushed deeper into her. He knew he had her now.

Bitch, you ain't going nowhere.

***

After an hour of nonstop sex, Nita slumped back on the sofa and let out a deep sigh. She ran her fingers through her sweaty hair, hating herself for letting her sexual desires get the best of her again. But then she thought to herself, *I don't care. I can have my cake and eat it too. That's what 3B does.*

"Getty-Gat, you don't mind if I take a shower, do you?" Nita asked.

"Nah. You know where it is."

Nita shoved herself off the sofa and left.

"Ava, won't you go join her," said Getty.

"Sure, dad." Ava kissed him on the cheek and pushed herself to her feet for a second round with Nita.

Getty-Gat fired up a cigarillo and sunk back into the sofa, switching on the flat screen TV. He wanted to check out the latest news in the music industry before Nita and Ava came back down from their shower. He flicked through the channels until he found *Music Bizz.* They were the source for all entertainment news.

"This just in: The founder and CEO of Wolfgang Records jumped from his hotel suite window. He has been pronounced dead on the scene." The blonde reporter seemed disturbed. "Also, acclaimed reporter Walter Fisher was shot and killed in a robbery in an underground garage. These are two horrible losses for the music industry."

Quickly, Getty-Gat sat up and snatched up his phone. He knew J-Money wouldn't want to hear about this but somebody had to tell him, if he didn't already know. Wolfgang Records was J-Money's cash cow, and with Herbert dead it might mark the end of their days in the drug business.

Chapter 17

Once Special Agent-in-Charge Day-Bailey explained their new assignment to them, Agent Sheryl Dunbar and Byron Avery headed to the city morgue to speak to the new agent they would be working with.

They were tasked with taking down the city's deadliest drug ring. This was just the case Agent Dunbar needed to correct the mistake she made in the Seymour Morgenstern case. She didn't want any mishaps with this one, so she told herself she'd play it by the book this time. She was anxious to meet with Agent Lori Albright. This gave Dunbar a chance to figure Albright out, make sure she was clear-headed. Albright had been undercover for two years, and after that amount of time most agents lost themselves mentally in their undercover personas. Dunbar needed to make sure Albright was still balanced.

Dunbar was wearing a brown Dolce & Gabbana sports jacket. The collar tickled her neck as she rolled it in circles, working out the kinks. She could barely contain her excitement—she had been given another chance to prove herself!

She walked alongside Avery into the examination lab, where Agent Albright was staring angrily into the lifeless brown eyes of a body lying on a metal table. It was Herbert Wolff's corpse. He had been Albright's shot to the top, and by him committing suicide shattered her chance to snap cuffs onto his wrists. She felt the two years she worked on his case was a waste of time.

"Hello, Agent Albright," said Dunbar.

Albright turned without a smile, but shook both Dunbar's and Avery's hands. "It's good to see you two. I'm glad to have you both on board."

"Same here," Dunbar said.

"It's a pleasure," said Avery with a huge goofy smile.

Dunbar cast Avery a side glance. She didn't want Avery making a fool out of them before they got the case underway.

"May we get started?" asked Albright, holding out a leather portfolio.

"Yes." Dunbar seized the portfolio and opened it up. "What do we got?"

"Here lies Herbert Wolff of Wolfgang Records. Earlier today he jumped from his hotel suite." Albright handed Dunbar more paperwork to add to the portfolio. "The examiner ruled it as a suicide after finding no signs of a murder."

"From this file, I see that Mr. Wolff is connected to three other suspects. So do these guys make up our drug ring?" Dunbar asked.

Albright set out three photos, pointing to each image one by one. "Aaron Ullman, Salvatore Barozzi, and Jermaine Irons. Aaron Ullman is the founder of Uman Records, Jermaine 'J-Money' Irons is the owner of Gatz Records, and Salvatore Barozzi is the boss of the Barozzi crime family."

Avery shared a little bit of his knowledge. "The Barozzi crime family is one of the oldest Mafia families in the world," he said. "They've been virtually untouched by us or any department internationally."

Albright nodded in agreement.

"How does this ring link together?" Dunbar asked.

"Aaron Ullman was the person with the drug connection. Salvatore Barozzi was the street connection, and Jermaine Irons and Herbert Wolff distributed the drugs. We are certain of this, but we just don't have enough evidence. And how they get the drugs out to their clientele is still a mystery to us. I was close to getting that information before Mr. Wolff kissed the pavement."

"Do we still stand a chance of taking down the others, without Wolff?" Dunbar asked.

"*Yes*," Albright said emphatically. "With the death of Mr. Wolff, we now have the wife, Chloe Wolff, taking over the record label." She showed them a photo of the widow.

"Me and Chloe have built a pretty good relationship since working this case. I think I can get what we need out of her."

"Do you think she knew about her husband's part in the drug operation?" Avery asked.

"Yes. She's sleeping with Mr. Irons. I'm certain he has told her all about the entire enterprise."

"Well that sums everything up," Dunbar said, collecting the photos and stuffing them back in the portfolio. "I guess we start first thing in the morning."

Chapter 18

After a long sip of his coffee, Almas returned his gaze to his laptop. He had spent the better part of the night running background checks on his artists and staff. He needed this transition to go smoothly. In order to assure this, background checks were necessary to avoid any unexpected problems that could force him to employ his skills as a hitman.

He was treating the move as head of Wolfgang Records as if he was preparing for a hit. That was how he had been trained to approach everything in life. It kept him safe and out of prison.

"Almas, I have all the contracts done," Nathan said.

"Good. All we're waiting for now is Randal, then we can go," Almas replied, closing the laptop shut.

The garage door slid open and in walked a six foot six, muscular built man. He came to a stop at the table where Almas and Nathan sat. He folded his hands in front of him and awaited a command like a well-trained K-9.

Nathan's gaze fell upon the dark, emotionless eyes of Randal Duncan and shivered as a chill crept up his spine. Randal Duncan was a hitman Almas brought in on jobs that required his special skills with explosives. He was a perfect fit for head of security. He had a knack for solving problems with discretion, and he was the best replacement if Almas was called on for another job.

"It's good to be working with you, Randal," Almas said with his hand held out.

Randal shook it. "Same here," he replied.

Almas picked up a pair of Ray-Ban sunglasses matching his tan Canali suit and placed them on. He rose to his feet and gave Randal a firm pat on the back. Randal was ex-military with a masters in the art of killing. He had honed this skill during his years carrying out black ops missions. With his particular skillset he was Almas's first choice to watch his back on this new venture.

"Since we're all here now," said Almas, "it's best we get this started."

Nathan stuffed his laptop and tablet into the Louis Vuitton backpack and headed toward his souped-up Mazda Rx-7. Almas tossed his coffee cup in the trash and slid his hand into his pocket for his keys as he approached his midnight black Porsche 911.

Randal shoved open the garage door and stepped to the side as they drove out of the garage.

***

The receptionist ended her phone call abruptly when she caught sight of who she assumed was the new owner of Wolfgang Records. She had received a call first thing this morning saying he would be here at 9 o'clock. She glanced at her watch to see he was timelier than her former boss. She snatched up her tablet and approached him.

"Good morning, Mr. Branson. Everybody is here, as you requested."

"Thank you. Yolanda Boman, right?" Almas asked.

"Yes." Yolanda extended her arm toward the conference room. "Please, this way."

Almas, Nathan, and Randal followed Yolanda to the conference room.

"Mr. Branson, would you and your associates like any beverages?" Yolanda asked.

"No thank you," Almas said.

"A Red Bull, please," Nathan said, taking her up on her offer.

Randal stared coldly at Yolanda and let out a grunt.

Nervously, Yolanda cut her gaze away, taking Randal's response as a no. "Oh-kay … Here we go, Mr. Branson." She opened the glass door.

Wolfgang Records' entire roster looked on at Almas as he pulled off his shades, stuffing them into breast pocket. He had an elegant but confident walk that made all present take notice. He was about business and exemplified that to a tee.

He walked to the head of the dark red oak table. Nathan and Randal accompanied him, and they had a seat on either side of him while he still remained standing.

"Let me start off by introducing myself," Almas began. "My name is Almas Branson. The new owner of Wolfgang Records."

Everybody looked to one another, shocked by his announcement. Trey "3B" Bryant, Charlie "Charlie Hustle" Owens, Gina Rogers, Philip "Phibo" Bowie, Kirara, Emily— every one of them was speechless.

"I know this comes as a little bit of a shock, but this is an opportunity for us all to become rich beyond our wildest dreams. On the same token, those who don't want to embrace this transition, you can leave now with your masters and you'll receive no ill will on my part." Almas glanced around the table at all of Wolfgang Records' artists. No one budged. He continued. "Good. Loyalty is what makes a new business venture function in a productive manner." He extended his hand to Nathan. "This is my assistant Nathan Branson. He will pass out the new contracts. Ms. Boman, could you bring in our attorney."

Yolanda nodded. "Yes, Mr. Branson," she said and stepped out into the hallway.

"I called in the attorney to answer any questions you might have about your contracts." Almas pulled out the leather swivel chair and sat down. "I'm in the business of making money. In order for me to do that we must all be of one accord. I put together a list for everybody's album release date. I want the summer to be flooded with our shit." Nathan handed Almas a sheet of paper, then passed the same one out to everybody at the table. "Trey Bryant, can you have your album complete in two weeks? The blog sites have been blowing up about your highly-anticipated album. And with the streets being unaware of your release from prison, it would position Wolfgang Records to lock up the streets for the summer."

Uncomfortably, Trey readjusted his hand underneath his chin, stunned by what Almas had said. One of the reasons he lied about his release date was to give him time to stack his money, leave Wolfgang Records and start his own label. Herbert was robbing him blind. That's why Trey didn't release an album before going to prison.

Trey just hoped when the time came, Almas let him go without any problems.

"Yeah," said Trey. "I can make that happen with the right team of producers."

Almas chuckled, picking up on what 3B was trying to do. Wolfgang Records had a reputation for employing the same, talentless producers. Almas knew all about 3B's plans to leave and he wanted to keep him part of the team. The only way he could achieve this was by making him happy. With Trey satisfied, the others would be more inclined to stay as well.

He motioned to Nathan, who pulled a sheet of paper from his portfolio and walked down to 3B. Nathan handed him the list of the industry's top producers. Almas glanced at his watch and looked to 3B, smiling. "They all will be here around eleven today."

Trey stared at the list in surprise. The ten names on the list were indeed the hottest in the country. There were a couple of them that Trey had planned on using for his new album. Seeing this, he began to wonder exactly who the hell Almas was.

"I hope these producers are to your liking," said Almas with a smile, seeing everybody staring at him excitedly.

"Yeah," was all Trey mumbled, and the rest agreed too.

"Good." Almas looked to Charlie Hustle. "Your album is next to drop after 3B's, then Gina Rogers, Phibo, and last but not least, Kirara. So, for the next month and a half, you will be in the studio. Do you guys and girls agree with this move?"

"Hell yeah," they all said in their own way, almost at once.

"That's what I want to hear. Now there is one more thing ..." Almas held his hand toward Randal. "This is the head of security, Randal Duncan. He will be assigning you a security team. Any problem you're faced with, let him and his team handle it. I don't want your partners or homeboys to handle *nothing*. Only Randal. Do I make myself clear?"

Everyone nodded in agreement.

"Since it's your album, Trey, that will reestablish us in this game, you will take the lead. Nathan will be assisting you as well."

"Let's hit the studio to get started," Trey said impatiently, pushing himself to his feet. He headed out of the conference room without another word. Everyone else followed him out.

Straggling behind, the receptionist Yolanda Boman quickly phoned her cousin, senior reporter for the *Scoop News*, Claire Collins.

"Hey, cousin. You won't believe what just happened ..."

Chapter 19

Clair hung up her phone and stuffed it in her pocket. The news from Yolanda was the type of scoop she loved to hear, but she had to focus her attention on the task at hand. She had to find out why Walter Fisher was killed.

She lifted up the mat where he kept his spare key. She unlocked the door and entered the studio apartment.

The place had been ransacked, confirming her suspicion about Walter's untimely death. It wasn't a random robbery gone bad—he had been targeted by a professional killer.

She headed over to the desk. Walter's laptop was missing. She opened the top drawer, no longer concerned with the missing computer; she reached inside. There was a *click*, and the desktop opened. She peeled off the flashdrive taped to it. The secret compartment was where Walter hid things he didn't want found.

Claire stuffed the flashdrive in her purse and quickly headed for the door. She wanted to get out of here, just in case whoever ransacked Walter's apartment returned for a second search.

***

Detective Bosco's eyes followed the young woman racing out of Walter's apartment to her car. Bosco was parked across the street. He grabbed his smartphone off the dashboard and snapped shots of her before she climbed into her car and pulled off. Last time Bosco was here—which was the night he killed Walter Fisher—he didn't find what he was looking for. But he knew someone would come sniffing around and find it for him. He needed to find out this woman's identity, so he could discover exactly what she took from Walter's apartment and why it had her rushing off in a hurry.

Bosco started up the department-issued Dodge Charger and drove off, bringing up J-Money's number to fill him in on what he just stumbled upon.

***

J-Money eased his phone in the inside pocket of his Prada sports jacket and headed over to the table where Salvatore and Aaron waited. He pulled out a chair and sat down.

"Some breakfast?" Salvatore asked, wiping his hands clean with a towel, then dropping it into his half-eaten plate of hard-boiled eggs and toast.

"Nah, I'm good," J-Money said.

"What's the situation?" asked Aaron after a sip of his glass of orange juice.

J-Money eased back in the chair and crossed his leg over his lap. "It seems Herbert sold Wolfgang Records to a Mr. Almas Branson. Farook was able to dig up a little bit of information on him. This Almas Branson has apparently made millions in the stock market."

"At least we know he likes making money," said Salvatore. "All we need to know now is, Will he be a team player?"

Aaron nodded. "Right you are, my friend. If he doesn't check out, he might be working for the Feds. This might be a trap. We need to approach this lightly."

"That's why I'm willing to pay him a visit. Just to feel him out," said J-Money.

Salvatore said, "Great idea. And if he isn't who he says he is, we'll just buy him out with a nice cozy retirement plan."

"I don't have a problem with that plan," Aaron said.

"Me either." J-Money stood and buttoned up his sports jacket. "Let me get going so I can meet our new friend. I'll call later and let you marvelous fellas know the outcome."

Chapter 20

For six hours strong, Trey "3B" Bryant spit verse after verse. Almas couldn't believe how talented 3B was. And it wasn't just him—everybody on Wolfgang Records' roster was gifted. Almas may have hit a gold mine on this deal.

Over the years his handler, Ellison Eaton, had hooked him up with many deals that made him a millionaire, not just his earnings as a contract killer. But this particular deal—CEO of Wolfgang Records—could be more profitable than any other deal Ellison had ever presented to him.

Almas leaned forward and pressed the speaker button that let him communicate with 3B inside the booth. "Let's break for a moment and get something to eat."

"A'ight," Trey said.

"Randal, call up Yolanda and tell her to order lunch," Almas said over his shoulder.

Randal picked up the receiver beside the door when it suddenly opened and Yolanda entered the studio.

"Mr. Branson, you have a guest," Yolanda announced.

"Who is it?"

"Jermaine Irons of Gatz Records," Yolanda answered, a little surprised herself. In the four years she had been working at Wolfgang Records, this was the third time she had ever seen Jermaine "J-Money" Irons. Though Herbert and Jermaine were well acquainted, J-Money very seldom visited. It made sense to Yolanda because some of Wolfgang and Gatz Records' artists were rivals.

"Show him to the conference room," said Almas. "I'll meet him there in a minute."

"Yes, Mr. Branson." Yolanda quickly exited the studio. She couldn't wait to tell her cousin about this meeting.

Almas rose to his feet and grabbed his suit jacket off the back of his chair. He slid it on and pulled his necktie snug. He had no need to ask who Jermaine Irons was. Until the wee hours of the morning he poured over information that Ellison Eaton had forwarded him, and he was able to brief himself on known and little-known facts about the music industry, including beefs with artists. Gatz Records was Wolfgang Records' biggest competition. For a couple years they had been battling for the top spot of the music game.

What really made this visit unexpected was the feud between 3B and a couple of the artists from J-Money's record label. It was one of the issues Almas found while he searched the background of 3B. Their rivalry was why Randal had been brought on as security. He wouldn't let Gatz Records *or* 3B disrupt the cashflow he was certain Wolfgang Records would be bringing in. Though Almas's earnings as a professional killer had him living comfortable, he was no different from any other for-profit investor—the more, the merrier.

Almas got Nathan's attention, motioning his cousin over.

Nathan excused himself from the group of producers and walked over to where Almas stood.

"What's up, cuzz?" Nathan asked.

With a slight roll of his neck, Almas stared coldly at Nathan. He hated when Nathan spoke like they were some sort of street niggas. "I need you to find out what kind of business ties J-Money and Herbert had exactly."

"What are you thinking?"

"I'll explain it to you later, after this visit from J-Money. I want to learn as much as I can about his intentions."

"He's here?!" Nathan exclaimed. After what he and Almas had read on J-Money last night, J-Money was one of three people that Almas was curious to know more about. They hadn't found any precise connection to J-Money and Herbert. This was just one of the few questions that went unanswered during their background checks.

"Yes," Almas answered. "That's why I want you to find out more about these business ties."

"Don't worry about it, I'm on top of it." Nathan patted Almas on the back and headed over to his backpack.

Almas stuffed his hands in his pockets and strolled out of the studio.

***

With the shoo of her hand, Chloe Wolff dismissed the maid and took a sip from the glass of freshly squeezed orange juice. She picked up her phone resting on her lap and brought up Herbert's attorney's number. She swung her autumn brown-colored hair over her shoulder and lifted the phone to her ear. "Hello, Shaman, it's me. I'll be at your office at one o' clock to sign whatever papers I need to."

Shaman knew what Chloe was referring to. He had warned Herbert of his young wife's intentions when they married. His friend Herbert finally took heed to his warning and changed his will seven months ago. He was about to take pleasure in breaking the news to Chloe. "Mrs. Wolff, there is no need for you to come down ..." He paused to keep from laughing. "It seems Herbert sold Wolfgang Records before he died."

"He what?!" Chloe screamed, sitting up in the lounge chair.

"You won't inherit Wolfgang Records."

"Motherfucka!" Chloe slammed her phone to the ground, shattering it into pieces. She wasn't about to let Herbert—or whoever he had sold the company to—screw her.

She jumped to her feet and stormed into the house to get herself ready for war.

***

As the glass door of the conference room opened and Almas strolled in, J-Money rose from the leather chair at the head of the table with his hand held out. "Mr. Branson, it's a pleasure to meet you."

"And you, Mr. Irons." Almas shook J-Money's hand and took a seat at the end of the table. "What do I owe the honor of this visit?"

"I'm extending a helping hand to you, since you're new to this business," J-Money said.

"Thank you. That would be much appreciated. You can either rise or fail in this business, *any business*, if you make a costly mistake. Any help is welcomed."

They jumped right into talks about certain aspects of the music industry, with J-Money giving his insight into creating "sticky" singles that listeners tend to gravitate to. He also told Almas that he was willing to offer verses from

151

his artists for free if he could get the same in return. Almas agreed, but this wasn't the "help" that Almas was looking for.

Almas pushed himself to his feet. "Mr. Irons, I hate to be rude by cutting your visit short, but I need to get myself familiar with some new producers we're beginning to work with. I would like you to attend 3B's album release party."

"I'll be there." J-Money stood.

"Okay. Yolanda will text you the information. Let me walk you out." Almas extended his arm toward the glass door.

J-Money buttoned up his sports jacket and let Almas lead him out of the conference room. Though Almas didn't expose much about himself, the one thing J-Money was able to pick up on was that Almas knew he and Herbert were more than rivaling record labels. But the exact extent of their relationship Almas had no idea of. He hoped Almas didn't dig too deep, for his sake. The book was still out on who Almas Branson really was. J-Money had faith in Farook on finding out answers. They couldn't just kill Almas Branson … until they learned whether or not he was a federal agent.

The doors leading into Wolfgang Records flew open and in strolled Chloe Wolff. Yolanda wanted to call security. By the look on Chloe's face, Yolanda could see her former boss's wife was pissed off that Wolfgang Records wasn't hers. She was here to raise hell.

Yolanda quickly got to her feet and approached Chloe. "Is there something I can help you with, Mrs. Wolff?"

"Yeah. I want to see the motherfucking owner."

"He's in a meeting at the moment. If you'll please wait, I'll get him when he's finished."

"No, I won't wait. Get his ass out here. Right now!"

"Yolanda, is there a problem?" Almas asked, staring at the woman trying to step around Yolanda. He didn't need his receptionist to tell him who the woman was. This was Chloe Wolff, Herbert's widow. She was a young, ambitious woman, wanting to make a name for herself by becoming head of Wolfgang Records. She was a problem that could shine a light on him that he didn't want.

J-Money stood by watching with his thumb in his pockets.

"You're my problem, you piece of shit," Chloe spat at Almas, as she stepped up to Almas and buried a manicured nail in his face. "You stole my record company from me, you sonofabitch. I suggest you call your lawyer up and prepare for war, because it's coming." Chloe threw an evil glance at J-Money, then pivoted on the balls of her feet and strutted toward the door.

"Mr. Branson, it was a pleasure meeting you," J-Money said, shaking off the shock of what just transpired.

"A pleasure for me as well," Almas replied.

J-Money shook Almas's hand and headed to the door. After the stunt Chloe just pulled, J-Money was sure she would become a problem that could serve as a threat to their drug operation. He fetched his smartphone out of his pocket and scrolled for Farook's number. He wanted Chloe silenced immediately.

"Yolanda, could you order lunch for us?" Almas asked.

"Yes, Mr. Branson."

"Also, I don't want to be disturbed by any unexpected visitors."

"Sure thing, sir."

Almas turned and headed toward the studio. It seemed he would have to dig deeper into the Wolfgang Records' background. He wanted to know what else he should expect to come his way.

Chapter 21

Stunned, the butler stared around the study littered with paper. In the six years he had been employed by the Wolffs, he had never seen Chloe exhibit this kind of determination toward anything.

When Chloe looked up from the papers she was browsing through and saw the butler staring at her, she snapped her fingers to get his attention. "Hey! What is it?"

"I'm sorry for disturbing you, Mrs. Wolff, but the evening meal is ready."

"Okay. You can bring it in here. This is where I'll be eating this evening."

"Yes, madam." The butler bowed slightly, then headed out of the study.

Chloe sunk back in the leather chair, tapping her nails on the desktop. She had to think of a way to get her record label from Almas Branson.

***

The cool breeze blowing off the pond felt soothing against Farook Hall's face as he fixed his gaze toward the mansion several feet away. He reached into his pocket and pulled out a redesigned smartphone. A friend who supplied him with all of his equipment also designed this phone; it was a nifty device that enabled him to hack into anybody's home security system, the perfect device for this kind of job. He didn't want anyone to be aware of his presence, especially the woman he was here to neutralize.

With the push of a button—*Beep!*—he deactivated the security system.

***

The butler entered the study carrying a tray with Chloe's evening dinner. He sat the tray on the end table and turned to Chloe. "Will that be all, Mrs. Wolff?"

"Yes, Gregory. I won't be needing you for the rest of the evening."

"Well, goodnight, madam."

Chloe waved off the butler and returned her focus back to Herbert's will.

"I see you're hard at work," Farook said as he strolled into the study.

Chloe looked up stunned to see Farook in her house. "How the hell you get in here?"

"Come on, Chloe. It's me you're talking about."

"You need to get the hell out of here," Chloe said loudly, in hopes that Gregory would here. She stood up.

"Now, Chloe. There's no need for all that yelling. You know if I wanted you dead, you would be." Farook walked over to the mini bar. "Please sit."

Nervously, Chloe did what she was told and sat down. What Farook said was true—if he wanted her dead, she probably wouldn't have even seen it coming. There was nothing she or Gregory would have been able to do to stop it.

"Since you aren't here to kill me," she said, "then why are you here?"

Farook slipped a small white pill into the glass of brandy he was preparing for her. It was a drug that would cause her to have a massive heart attack. The drug was untraceable. Her toxicology screening would come back clean.

After pouring himself a glass of brandy, he handed the spiked glass to Chloe and took a seat in a leather bucket seat. "J-Money said he saw you at Wolfgang Records complaining. He sent me to talk to you."

"Why didn't that traitor come himself?"

"Really? You need to ask?"

She shrugged her shoulders. "What does he want?"

"He wants you to back down. He has a plan to get your record company for you, if you would just chill."

"Really?" She looked hopeful.

"Yeah." Farook downed his drink and rose to his feet. "Will you behave yourself?"

"No doubt ... if he can help me."

"He *is* helping you." Farook headed out of the study. "I'll leave this glass in the kitchen. You have a good evening."

"You too. And tell J-Money I said thank you."

"Will do." Farook waved goodbye, then disappeared into the hallway.

Chloe drank the remainder of her glass of brandy and suddenly paused, struck by a sharp chest pain. She slowly stood, clutching her bosom. She began to panic as she struggled to breathe. *What's happening? I need help!* "Gregory ..." she cried out.

The butler's name faded from her lips as she dropped to the floor dead.

***

Farook switched on the security system—*Beep-beep!*—then stepped through the bushes. The pill he had slipped in Chloe's drink was fast-acting. By the time the butler got to her or discovered her, she would be long dead, exactly the way J-Money wanted.

Chloe Wolff would be completely out of the picture.

His next task was preparing to remove J-Money's other obstacle, Mr. Almas Branson himself.

Chapter 22

Heavy bass rumbled out of the rear of the ebony black 2017 Cadillac Escalade ESV, pulling to a screeching stop in front of Gatz Records. The passenger door opened and a six foot eight giant in a black suit exited the vehicle. He opened the rear door and folded his hands in front of him.

Frank "Frankie" White emerged from the cocaine white leather seats of the Escalade ESV. He jacked up his navy blue khakis and adjusted the St. Louis Rams ballcap, then started up the walkway leading to the doors of Gatz Records. He was a rapper who fell out of the Northside of St. Louis. Before becoming a multi-platinum rapper, he was a street dealer, pushing drugs all throughout the country, whatever state was booming. He wasn't a heavy-hitter in the game, but he wasn't a struggling dealer either. His hustle game was what attracted J-Money. Frankie and his crew members, Getty-Gat and Pow-Wow, got signed to Gatz

Records soon after. Since then, they had been the biggest contributors to J-Money's record company and his illegal operation.

Pow-Wow stepped out of the Cadillac next, his face buried in his smartphone. Despite him being only a year younger than Frankie, he acted a lot younger. Frankie had to constantly remind him that he was in a great position as a rap artist and he needed to take his career serious.

Frankie turned to him. "I swear to God, at the slightest sign that you're bullshitting, I promise you your ass won't be on this album."

"A'ight, nigga. I got you. So chill."

For a moment Frankie White stared coldly at Pow-Wow, driving home his point with silent intimidation. When Pow-Wow sighed and stuffed his phone in his pocket, Frankie White spun around and headed into the building.

***

J-Money studied the dark-skinned woman sitting in the arm-chair. Her name was Sunila Jones. She had less-than-cute features that reminded him of a stripper he once knew. But what she lacked in looks she made up for in her voluptuous frame. Sunila Jones wasn't signed for her appearance though. It was her voice. She had one of the most soulful voices he had ever heard. For that reason, he kept her on the label.

"Sunila, how you looking on your album?" J-Money asked.

Sunila looked up from her phone. "It's coming along nicely."

"Coming along isn't good enough. I want you to have your album wrapped up by the end of the week."

"What's the rush?" Sunila asked.

"I need your album to be out before Gina Rogers's hits the streets."

Sunila dug her nails into the arms of her chair. She couldn't stand the ground Gina walked on. They grew up in the same housing projects. Sunila and her friends always picked on Gina because of her pretty looks. It wasn't until they got into their teens her hatred for Gina grew deeper. While Gina's looks kept local hustlers buying her the latest designer clothes and the newest cars, Sunila spent her time earning a living the hard way—by selling drugs. Even when it came to record contracts, Gina's was better than hers. She knew she had to end Gina's career with her latest album.

"I'll have my album wrapped up by the end of the week," Sunila promised.

"That's what I wanted to hear," J-Money said. He looked up toward the door as it opened. Frankie White, Pow-Wow, and Getty-Gat strolled into the office. "Finally, everybody is here."

"What's up, J-Money?" Frankie White said.

J-Money eased back in his seat and folded his hands in his lap. "Everybody needs to start wrapping up their albums in the next couple weeks."

"Why?" Getty-Gat asked.

"It seems like we have more than 3B as a problem now. We have to add the new owner of Wolfgang Records to the list, some wannabe bigshot named Almas Branson." J-Money sat forward, resting his hands on the desktop. "That's why we need to go hard on your upcoming album, to blow these chumps out of the water." He slammed a firm finger on the desk.

Frankie White wiped the corner of his mouth, bringing his gaze up to meet J-Money's. "You best believe these niggas' end is coming real soon."

"Exactly what I want to hear," J-Money said with a devious smirk, as he reclined back in his seat.

Chapter 23

Steam rolled off the cup of coffee as Almas took a sip. Today was Herbert Wolff's funeral. He hadn't planned to attend but felt he needed to for the sake of his artists. Also, attending the funeral would give him a chance to meet all of the players.

"Almas, the limo is here," Randal said, entering Almas's office.

Almas picked up the remote control off his desk and switched off the huge flatscreen TV, then followed Randal out the door.

***

Where Agent Byron Avery had the van parked, it gave them a clear view of the church. At the same time it kept them out of sight from those attending Herbert Wolff's funeral. They didn't want any of their suspects to know they were being investigated by the FBI.

When Agent Sheryl Dunbar noticed a limousine pull up and a swarm of reporters began to gather around the vehicle, she elbowed her partner in the arm. "Take a look at that," she said.

Agent Avery was enjoying a cup of coffee. He sat it in the cup holder, then picked up the camera off of his lap. He began to snap shots of the woman climbing from the limousine. "Who do you think she is?"

"I don't know. Give me a second and I'll tell you." Dunbar ran her fingers across the keys of the laptop resting in her lap. The camera Avery held was connected to her laptop, which was linked to the FBI's database.

She stared strangely at the screen.

"Look." She turned to Avery so he could see the word *denied* flashing red on the screen. "We only have one option now …"

"Yeah, we're gonna have to have Lewis Day-Bailey get us access."

"Right," Dunbar sighed. "Let's finish up so we can get back and find out what the hell is up with our mystery woman."

Agent Avery began to snap more shots as another limousine pulled up. *Click-click-click!*

***

Chanel sunglasses with black mirror lenses slid over Samantha Wolff's hazel eyes as the limousine pulled up to the gothic-style church. Her personal bodyguard, Malik, exited the limousine and helped her out onto the sidewalk, where she took a quick look up at the clear blue sky, as if asking God himself for permission to enter one of His homes. Reporters quickly gathered around her, throwing nonstop questions at her.

Samantha ignored all of them and headed up the limestone steps without missing a beat. She wasn't here to answer questions; she was here to identify her enemies.

The usher was beginning to lead everybody up the aisle to view the body when Samantha took a seat on the pew in the first row. She studied the people who viewed Herbert's body and who came over to her to give their condolences. What her personal bodyguard Malik told her echoed in her mind. *Somebody attending the funeral is responsible for your father's murder,* he had said to her vehemently. *They're gonna show their face. Just watch and see.* He didn't believe her father committed suicide, and neither did she. She had Malik look into her father's death. He discovered that Herbert's business partners were planning to kill him. Then, as if to add more evidence to their theory, a strange man named Almas Branson just so happened to purchase Wolfgang Records just before the alleged suicide.

To call all of this questionable was an understatement. Samantha wasn't buying it. They—whoever *they* was—had murdered her father! And they would all pay dearly for it.

"I won't rest until your killer is dead, daddy," Samantha whispered to herself, as she glared at Salvatore, Aaron, and J-Money making their way over to her. She put on a fake smile and welcomed their cold hugs.

UP NEXT:

STREET MOGULS
AND
MAFIA BOSSES 2

Text **JORDAN** to **77948**

And stay updated on all of Jordan Belcher Presents' *newest releases, free giveaways,* and *special promotions!*

BCPL
Baltimore County
Public Library

CPSIA information can be obtained
at www.ICGtesting.com
Printed in the USA
LVOW08s2037110117
520606LV00001B/40/P

9 781541 372153